HAPPILY EVER AFTERLIFE

AFTERLIFE

School Spirit

HAPPILY EVER
AFTERLIFE

HAPPILY EVER AFTERLIFE

School Spirit

by Orli Zuravicky

SCHOLASTIC INC.

ISBN 978-1-338-19300-8

10 9 8 7 6 5 4 3 2 1   17 18 19 20 21
Printed in the U.S.A.   40
First printing 2017

Book design by Jennifer Rinaldi

To Mia, Jonah, and Lucy
my little inspirations

THE LIMBO SPIRIT CARNIVAL RULES

RULE #1:

The annual Limbo Spirit Carnival is an opportunity to show your school spirit! This is a wonderful way to engage in some good, healthy competition, and we hope you embrace it while having fun doing something charitable for your school.

Chapter One
Got Spirit?

The last time I waited in the administration office this early in the morning for my guidance counselor, Ms. Keaner, was the day I crossed over.

My ghostday, if you will.

I was twelve shades of anxious (not to mention completely see-through!), and I kept falling through the waiting-room chair while my soon-to-be nemesis, Georgia Sinclaire, hurled insults at me like it was her job.

Good times.

But boy, how *times* have changed!

(And I don't just mean the fact that my state of solidity is one hundred percent!)

That's right. Not only am I capable of doing multiple toddler-level activities, like scratching my nose without missing my face (hooray!), but I'm apparently one of the most advanced new ghosts at Limbo Central Middle School. At least, that's what Miles Rennert said when I told him about my telepathic abilities last week. (Telepathy is when you can read someone else's mind. Crazy, right?!) Anyway, Miles is a third year here, and he's a telepath, too, which is apparently a very rare skill.

He's also super cute.

And a musician.

And it seems likely that he has a teeny-weeny crush on me, but at this point that information is completely and totally irrelevant, because as of three days ago, I officially started dating Mr. Perfect Ghost Boy Year Two ex-tutor, aka picture-perfect, adorably dimple-faced, makes-my-stomach-jump-every-time-I-see-him Colin Reed.

And I have absolutely no regrets about that.

None whatsoever.

Cross my heart and hope to beat.

Swear on my own grave.

Though I'm not entirely sure that counts, since I'm not really dead in the traditional sense of the word. I mean, I'm dead but I'm, like, *here*. I'm dead *alive*, not dead *dead*.

You know what I mean.

My point? Last week I chose Colin over Miles, and a decision is a decision. I've had a crush on Colin since the day I got here. Something about the way he smiles at me and makes me feel like I'm the first person to really *get* him makes my knees weak. From the moment I first saw him, I fell for him.

I also *literally* fell, like, flat ON MY FACE.

But that's a different story.

That's why, even though Miles and I have a connection, too, I know in my gut that Colin is it. It's, like, fate.

So, that's that.

Getting back to what I was saying before, being a ghost definitely has its perks. Like being able to hear what other people are thinking, for one, even though I'm *supposed* to be learning how to block people out by building my Wall—a psychological protection system that ghosts can create to keep people like me out of their heads. It's supposed to help me keep their voices out, too, because technically I shouldn't be listening. That's just one of the GAZILLION rules about being a telepath in the afterlife and at Limbo Central.

Not that that's even remotely surprising.

That's why I'm here, actually. Because I HAVE to tell someone about what's going on and—

"Lucy, Ms. Keaner will see you now!" Ms. Lyons, the secretary, sings with a smile on her face. "Look at you. You're advancing so quickly! Didn't I tell you you'd get the hang of it sooner or later, doll?"

I stand up and head into Ms. Keaner's office, offering Ms. Lyons a smile.

"Good morning, Lucy!" Ms. Keaner says, ushering me in. "To what do I owe this early-morning visit?"

"Hi, Ms. Keaner," I say, taking a seat. "So, I have something I think I should tell you."

"Oh, dear, is something wrong?"

"No, no," I say, but I suddenly feel myself getting nervous. "It's just, well . . . I've discovered that I'm telepathic."

"You're what, dear?"

"Telepathic. You know, I can, like, read people's thoughts?"

"Yes, yes, of course I know what telepathic means. I just . . . well, I suppose I'm a little surprised. It's been quite some time since someone has reported that particular ability to me. But, then again, this does seem somewhat fitting. You've been surprising us at every turn, haven't you, Lucy?"

I shrug sheepishly, trying to stop myself from blushing.

"If you don't mind, Lucy, dear, would you please demonstrate this skill for me, so I can see for myself? I'm going to let my Wall down, and . . . oh my, do you know what the Wall is?"

"Yes, I know what the Wall is," I confirm.

"Oh, good. Okay, so now I'm going to let mine down, and you tell me what it is that I'm thinking."

Ms. Keaner closes her eyes, and suddenly I hear a familiar whooshing sound, like someone has just opened the window in a car going sixty miles an hour on the highway. See, ever since I opened the floodgates of my mind, there's been this constant rush of white noise from people's thoughts. If I'm around a lot of adults (like in this office), it's usually pretty quiet, because they obviously have their Walls up—just like

Ms. Keaner usually does—so I can't hear them. But at school, around the students, especially the kids in Years One and Two, it's SUPER noisy. If I'm distracted by something, it's easier to block out the noise. But once I start listening, forget about it.

Suddenly, I hear Ms. Keaner's voice shoot through my head:

She sells seashells by the seashore,
by the seashore he sells seashells.

Uh . . . what was *that*?

"Um, Ms. Keaner, do you *really* want me to repeat that?"

"Yes, please go ahead."

"Okay . . . you thought, 'She sells seashells by the seashore, by the seashore he sells seashells.' But didn't you mean 'she' instead of 'he'?"

"Magnificent!" she calls out. "And no, I did not. I must call Mr. Nasser in here at once. Just hold on a moment, dear."

Then Ms. Keaner opens the door to her office and calls out, "Ms. Lyons, please phone Mr. Nasser and tell him to come in here at once, thank you!"

Three minutes of twiddling my thumbs later, the Telepathy teacher comes charging into Ms. Keaner's office. He's breathing as if he's just run a marathon.

"What's the emergency?" he blurts out.

"No emergency, Mr. Nasser," Ms. Keaner says. "Did Gayle tell you it was an emergency? Gayle! Did you tell Mr. Nasser it was an emergency?"

Then, without waiting to hear the answer, Ms. Keaner shuts the door to her office.

"Mr. Nasser, we have some exciting news to share with you. Lucy Chadwick is exhibiting signs of telepathy!"

"My apologies, but it cannot be," Mr. Nasser remarks, smugly. "She is far too young and new to the afterlife."

"Well, be that as it may," Ms. Keaner says, "it is a reality. She has exhibited her abilities for me, and I can attest to them."

"May I see for myself?" he asks.

"Of course. Lucy, please show Mr. Nasser what you showed me a few moments ago."

I'm starting to feel like some circus freak, and stealthily check my chin to make sure I'm not spontaneously sprouting any facial hair. (You know, like the Bearded Lady, get it?)

Anyway, I suppose I should be used to this by now—it's not as if I've ever really been normal. Well, at least not since I first arrived here.

But this? Is nerve-racking.

"Okay, Ms. Chadwick, please go ahead and tell me what I'm thinking now," Mr. Nasser says.

How much wood could a woodchuck cut
if a woodchuck could cut wood?

Again?!

"Do I seriously have to say that out loud?" I plead.

This is getting embarrassing.

For all of us.

"Humor me," Mr. Nasser replies.

"Fine. 'How much wood could a woodchuck cut if a woodchuck could cut wood.' But it's actually, how much wood could a woodchuck CHUCK, not cut."

"Precisely!" Mr. Nasser says, standing up and shaking his finger triumphantly in the air, as if he's just caught me red-handed—doing what, I have absolutely no idea. "I changed the words to see how exact your reading would be. If a student actually does exhibit telepathic powers at your age and level, he or she would possibly be able to hear bits and pieces of my thoughts but rarely the whole thought. Therefore, they would *assume* they know the rest of the phrase without actually reading it."

"So . . . you just tried to trick me?"

"In a word," Mr. Nasser says, "yes."

"Ms. Keaner, did you try to trick me, too?" I ask.

"In a word," she replies, sheepishly, "yes."

I look at her and then him, shaking my head. "Sneaky."

"Yes, well, we'll need to get started on your lessons right away!" Mr. Nasser tells us. "Now, you haven't taken your placement examination yet, so the lessons will remain private until such time that you are officially placed in a ghost year. But there is another student here who shall join us, whose expertise you can benefit from. Please report to my classroom tomorrow afternoon at 3 P.M. to get started."

With that, he marches out of her office, perfectly in time with the first bell.

"You better get going to your first class," Ms. Keaner says.

"But don't worry about that placement-exam talk—you'll learn all about it when the time comes. I'm glad you came to talk to me, Lucy. These lessons are going to be so good for you! Now, run along to class and we'll talk more later."

Before I know what has hit me, Ms. Keaner shoos me out of her office, leaving me with about a thousand unanswered questions batting around in my head.

None of which have anything to do with the amount of wood a woodchuck can cut.

Or chuck.

Or upchuck. (Ha!)

"Wait, what did you just say about Georgia?" I ask my good friend Mia Bennett, biting into my pizza like I haven't eaten in three days.

It's finally lunchtime, and I'm ravenous.

What? Reading people's minds makes a ghost hungry. Jeez!

"I said that Ms. Sotherby told me Georgia was caught sneaking back into the dorm through the window on Saturday. After midnight. Georgia said she'd been helping Lexi

Landen with some kind of emergency." Mia makes quotations with her hands when she says the word "emergency," and I can tell she's irritated.

"So, when Georgia was *supposed* to be having a sleepover with us," Cecily Vanderberg (my afterlifelong best friend FOREVER) says, "a sleepover that *she* suggested, by the way, but then didn't show up for, she was *actually* running all over campus with this Lexi Landen person breaking curfew?"

"Affirmative," Mia replies.

"And who's Lexi Landen?" I ask.

"You don't know?" Briana Clark has a shocked expression on her face. "She's in Year Three. I thought *everyone* knew about her."

Cecily and I are still kinda new to Limbo Central. We obviously have *a lot* of gossip to catch up on.

"Okay, word on the street," says Oliver Rennert, our good friend and VP of the Limbos (that's our dance club), "is that Lexi Landen is a Class-A bad kid—so bad, in fact, that she got herself kicked out of North Limbo when she was in Year One. That's how she ended up here at Limbo Central second semester."

"She showed up right around the same time as Miles, didn't she, Oliver?" Briana asks.

Oliver and Miles are brothers, hence the sharing of their last name.

"Yes, but they didn't, like, know each other or anything," Oliver answers. "Miles said it was just a weird coincidence."

Suddenly, Colin, Trey Abbot (Mia's boyfriend), Marcus Riley (Cecily's boyfriend), Jonah Abbot (Trey's big brother), and a few guys slam their trays down like hulks at our table.

Boy invasion!

"Hello?" Oliver reprimands. "We're, like, right in the middle of a seriously important conversation? Do you mind keeping it down?"

This is one of the MANY reasons I heart Oliver to death. No pun intended.

"Anyway," Mia continues, "Lexi has a seriously bad reputation. She was always getting into trouble back at North Limbo, and now she's pulling Georgia down with her."

"Lexi Landen?" Trey asks, biting into his slice like he hasn't a care in the world. "She's not *that* bad. Kinda cool, actually."

Mia shoots him a look that could melt the cheese off his slice.

"What?" he says, shrugging his shoulders. "I'm just saying—"

"Maybe don't say that just now," I hint, trying to save him from himself.

He shoves his pizza farther into his mouth, and I turn to Mia.

"Georgia's a big girl. It's not your job to take care of her," I say, though I suppose I am a bit biased, considering that Georgia is literally the bane of my nonexistence. "It was her choice to hang out with Lexi and break curfew instead of hanging with us."

"You can't *really* blame her for not wanting to hang out with you though," Chloe McAvoy—Georgia's ex-bestie—says. She's referring to the fact that Georgia and I have almost never been on good terms, and we certainly weren't on the specific night in question.

It's a long story.

Fine . . . long story short? Colin used to be her boyfriend, but now he's mine, and Georgia hates me for it. I didn't mean for it to go down this way, but it's not like Georgia is some angel. I mean, she threw balls at my head multiple times, okay? Jeez, what's with the third degree?

Sorry. Emotional Girl rears her head again.

"No, I guess I can't exactly blame her," I agree with Chloe.

"But *I* can!" Cecily chimes in, smiling.

"Your loyalty is touching," I say.

"What are besties for?"

"So, is this girl, like, really bad news?" I ask, trying to get a read on the situation, even though I don't actually care either way where Georgia is concerned.

"Well, she's not good news," Mia concludes.

Just then, Principal Tilly approaches the stage, and the cafeteria falls silent.

"Hello, students of Limbo Central!" she trills into the microphone. "I'm up here today to announce some exciting news. Our annual Limbo Spirit Carnival will take place in two weeks on Saturday! This carnival is an excellent opportunity for both Limbo Central and North Limbo to do something wonderful for our fair town and to show our appreciation to our neighbors. It is also the perfect opportunity for you to showcase your school spirit! All students and clubs are encouraged to sign up for a booth or an event at the carnival, and the event that receives the highest spirit scores will win the sacred Limbo Spirit Cup! Additionally, all of the proceeds that are earned at the carnival will be donated to the winner's school, and the winning group will receive a front-page article in their school's newspaper. Finally, the winning group will also be allowed to designate a portion of the carnival earnings to the club or school event of their choice. Now, I must remind you to be on your very best behavior—no funny business with North Limbo will be tolerated this year! It would behoove you to remember that showing spirit for your school does not include showing disdain for someone else's. Now, let's make this the very best Limbo Spirit Carnival ever!"

With that, Ms. Tilly walks off stage, and the cafeteria is abuzz with chatter.

"Ugh, I can't stand North Limbo," Briana says before Ms. Tilly can even make it down the stairs. "Last year they won the Cup, and they haven't let us live it down since."

"So we have to KILL IT this year," Oliver agrees. "We cannot let those losers torment us for the second year in a row!"

"The losers of *North Limbo*?" I say, confirming who we're talking about.

"Obvi!" Oliver replies, irritated that he has to repeat himself.

"Just checking," I say. "So . . . North Limbo and Limbo Central are major rivals then, huh?"

"Duh!" Oliver cries. "I can't even *believe* you had to ask that."

"I'm already regretting it," I reply, winking at Cecily.

Cecily and I secretly LOVE it when Ollie gets all snotty and mean like a grouchy old person. It's HILARIOUS.

Another one of the MANY reasons why we heart Oliver.

Just then, Georgia and Lexi waltz past our table, laughing about something.

"That's her," Chloe whispers to me and Cecily.

Mia's eyes travel with them all the way across the cafeteria.

That's Lexi Landen?

I've totally seen this girl around campus before, but I had

no idea who she was until now. The moment I match the name with the face, I know exactly why Trey said what he said about her.

Lexi's not just pretty cool, she's, like, the reason the word was invented. (Not that I'm about to tell Mia that, and if anyone tells her I said so, I'll just deny it!)

One afternoon, about two weeks after I got here, I was gazing out the window during class when I noticed Lexi— though I didn't know who she was then—sitting with her back up against a tree, reading. I couldn't see what book it was because she was too far away, but something about the look on her face, how totally into it she was, stuck with me. She kept uncapping her pen and writing notes in the margins, and looking up at the sky as if she was deep in thought. A few minutes into watching her, a group of three other kids exited school and walked up to her. She slipped the book into the back pocket of her oversize corduroys and they all snuck off campus.

She's the kind of girl who can walk around in a pair of men's pants with a book in the back pocket and no one looks at her funny for it.

Today she's wearing worn-out overalls and a pair of Vans, and her long, light-brown hair is all perfectly beach-wavy, when on any other person it just would look unbrushed. She has this air of I-don't-care about her, which is basically impossible to have in middle school.

Believe me, I've tried.

Epic. Fail.

"Okay," Mia says, peeling her eyes off Lexi and Georgia and reentering the conversation. "You guys figure out a way to win the carnival, and I'll figure out a way to get Stacy Francis to give me that front-page beat—no matter what it takes."

"Done and done," Oliver says.

"I'm serious," Mia continues. "The stakes are high."

"I've never seen Mia care so much about winning a silly competition before," I whisper to Trey, when Mia isn't looking.

"This isn't just any competition," he replies. "Mia's been trying to get one of her articles on the front page of *The Limbolater* for the past year and a half, and Stacy Francis is always turning her down. Leading up to the carnival last year, Mia wanted to run an article about the pranks North Limbo and Limbo Central have played on each other over the years, and instead Stacy totally stole Mia's idea and wrote the article herself. She's the editor in chief, so she has final say over everything. At this point, it's personal."

Okay, these stakes? Just went through the roof.

School spirit, here we come.

The Limbo Spirit Carnival Rules

Rule #2:

The group that wins the Spirit Carnival wins the Spirit Cup in the name of their school. Said school is allowed to keep and display the Cup in any manner they choose for exactly one year, until the next Limbo Spirit Carnival, at which point the Cup shall be returned to the carnival committee the morning of the carnival for cleaning.

Chapter Two
The Wall

I can't believe it's already 2:45 on Tuesday afternoon.

The rest of Monday and Tuesday morning LITERALLY flew by like, well, a bird, or a plane, or anything that flies ridiculously fast while opposing gravity. With Ms. Tilly's Spirit Carnival announcement, the telepathy stuff, and trying to figure out what Georgia is going to do for the carnival with her cheer squad so I can make sure that the Limbos beat it, I haven't had much time to stop and breathe.

Luckily, ghosts don't need oxygen.

(Yet another afterlife perk. *Woot! Woot!*)

At least Colin and I had an AMAZING chat last night on our Tabulators. He told me all about the family ski vacations he used to go on every year, and how he chose snowboarding because he thinks that skiing is basically just walking through snow, and he does that all winter long. He keeps begging me to teach him how to surf, and I promised him I will as soon as the carnival is over.

Also, last night I *finally* told Cecily about my "powers." At first she was super psyched, but then I could sense her getting a little weirded out, wondering if I'd ever used my abilities to listen in on *her* thoughts, which led to a whole chorus of her asking, "Can you hear what I'm thinking now?" and "What about now?" that went on for like ten minutes.

Obviously I told her I couldn't and never had.

I know that's *technically* not the whole truth, but I didn't want to make her upset or uncomfortable. Also, *technically*, I never listened to her thoughts on purpose. That one time was an accident.

What? Accidents happen.

But that accident is never going to happen again, because at this very moment I'm on my way to Mr. Nasser's classroom for my first private lesson in building THE WALL.

It sounds like some kind of top secret government assignment, doesn't it?

Operation Build-the-Wall.

Okay, that just sounds C.R.E.E.P.Y.

Moving on . . . I'm a little early, but I'm actually looking forward to having a bit of quiet time before we start. You know, to align my chakras, and whatever else calm people do to stay that way.

"Hey," a voice says the second I round the corner into Mr. Nasser's classroom.

I jump back a little, startled.

The voice belongs to Miles.

That's right. Miles Rennert, aka Cute Year Three Musician Boy, the one I turned down to date Colin, is standing in Mr. Nasser's classroom waiting for what I can only assume will be our private lesson.

Together.

Just the two of us. (Well, and Mr. Nasser too.)

Reading each other's minds.

Just another normal day in the afterlife.

"Oh, hey," I reply, trying to downgrade my level of shock from completely unhinged to pleasantly surprised.

Total F.A.I.L.

So Miles is the other gifted student that Mr. Nasser was talking about earlier? I mean, I kind of knew that already, since Miles is the one who helped me discover my abilities last week. But there must be more than two people in this school who have this ability, right? I figured Mr. Nasser would pair me up with someone closer to my level of skill.

Apparently not.

"Mr. Nasser didn't tell me who I'd be working with," I continue.

"Sorry to disappoint."

"No, I didn't mean it like that," I reply, trying to change my tone.

I feel myself going downhill rapidly. If I were a car, a red light would appear on my dashboard flashing ENGINE FAILURE!

Abort, Lucy, abort!

"This is good, you know, since we already like each—I mean, work well together."

Your engine will self-destruct in three . . . two . . . one . . .

"Yeah," Miles says. "*Something* like that."

Uh . . . did you feel that? *Brrrrr*, it's cold in here.

(And it's not just because we're ghosts.)

"So . . . did you hear Ms. Tilly's announcement yesterday?" I ask, trying to lighten the mood.

"The one about the Spirit Carnival?"

"Yeah."

"Yup."

"What was all that talk about 'no funny business with North Limbo'? Do you know?"

"Kids are always playing pranks on the winning school, trying to steal the Cup and stuff. Two years ago, some kids from North Limbo broke into Limbo Central and played a stupid prank on the Spirit Cup. The whole thing's pretty ridiculous, if you ask me."

"The rivalry?"

"The rivalry. The pranks. The whole carnival. Competition makes people do stupid things."

"Do you know who pulled that Cup prank?"

Suddenly the sound of shuffling feet in the hallway pulls my attention away from Miles, just in time to see Georgia and Lexi pass by—but not without them first peering into the classroom to see exactly who is inside it.

"Well that's just *perfect*," I blurt out without thinking.

I wonder how long it will take Georgia to tell Colin some insane story about me and Miles meeting here in private behind his back?

Calling all skywriters—please report to Georgia McTattletale!

"What's wrong now?" Miles asks.

"It's just Georgia and that Lexi girl . . . "

"What do you have against Lexi?" he says, not exactly accusingly.

But not *NOT* accusingly.

"Well, the fact that she's hanging out with Georgia already tells me plenty about her character, I think."

"Right," Miles says, with an air of annoyance.

"What?" I ask.

"Nothing. I guess your high opinion of both of them makes them a perfect match for each other," he suggests.

"I guess it does," I reply, though I'm sensing there's something he's not saying. "Why? Do you know something about Lexi that I don't? Am I missing some important information that would make me completely change my mind about her?"

"There's always missing information," he says matter-of-factly. "But I doubt it would make you change your mind, since you've already made it up, and hey, a decision is a decision, right? And either you're right, and they are both as bad as they seem . . . "

"Or?"

"Or you're wrong, and maybe the problem is that you write people off a little too quickly. Maybe you're not as good at judging a person's character as you thought you were."

Ouch.

Okay, I know there aren't any balls in this classroom, so why does it feel like I just caught a fast one to the face?

"I . . . I guess—"

"Good, you're both here!" Mr. Nasser announces as he enters, saving me from having to finish my thought. "Miles knows how I feel about students being punctual. So, let us begin! Now, Lucy, the purpose of these lessons is to teach you how to build your Wall. And the purpose of the Wall for a ghost is twofold: First and foremost, its purpose is to protect your own thoughts from external intruders, or other telepaths. Second, its purpose is to help you block other ghosts' thoughts from bombarding you twenty-four hours a day."

I know I'm supposed to be paying attention to what Mr. Nasser is saying, but I can't stop thinking about what just happened with Miles. He's, like, the chillest person I've ever met, and yet out of nowhere he gets weirdly defensive and starts acting like we're in the middle of some verbal throw-down.

Lucy, 0. Miles, 1,000,000.

Does he actually think I'm a bad judge of character? And why does he care what I think of Lexi? Is there a reason he's defending her that I don't know about . . . Does he really think I write people off too quickly? Because that's, like, an awful thing to think about someone. Does he think I wrote *him* off too quickly when I chose Colin?

And what if he's right?! I mean, I didn't even know this Lexi person existed two days ago, and now I'm suddenly talking about her behind her back and acting like she's a Death Eater or something.

Grrr.

I'm so frustrated I could—

"Lucy?" Mr. Nasser calls, and I snap back to reality.

"Yes, sir."

"Can you please refrain from practicing your telekinesis skills in my classroom, thank you!"

"I, uh . . ."

Oh. My. Ghost.

I glance over behind his desk and notice that while my mind was losing it over what Miles said, Emotional Girl was taking great pleasure in writing DEATH EATER! in big block letters across the chalkboard.

Mortified, table for one.

"Sorry, Mr. Nasser, sir," I plead, running over to erase the board.

Out of the corner of my eye, I notice Miles smirking.

Ugh.

"As I was saying," Mr. Nasser continues, unfazed, "the more advanced you become, the more you will be able to manipulate your Wall. For example, you will be able to keep some layers of your Wall up whilst letting other layers down to breach someone else's, among many other things. But your first task is to build the basic structure of your Wall.

Now, the first step to building your Wall is to think of a place where you feel safe. Take a few minutes to think about that place."

A place where I feel safe? I guess I could choose my room, or my old house with the blue shutters and the wraparound porch? Or maybe I should pick something here . . . like the beach?

"Lucy, do you have your safe space?" Mr. Nasser asks.

"Yes, I have it."

"Very good. The key to building a strong Wall is in the details. I want you to imagine building this safe place you're picturing in your mind from scratch—as if you're an architect. Every detail of the space—the colors, the textures, the feel, the temperature, even the smell—is important. And the more of these details you include, the stronger your Wall will become."

"Okay."

"Are you ready to begin?" he asks me.

"Yes, I'm ready."

"Miles, please let down your Wall. Lucy, if you are constructing your Wall correctly, you won't be able to hear Miles's thoughts. If you can hear them, whatever you're doing isn't working, so you need to try something else. Okay? Ready, go!"

Great. I can build a beach. Piece of cake. What do beaches need? Waves crashing. Soft, warm sand. Hot sun. Okay . . . what else . . . what else . . .

Okay you were right, there is a reason I'm defending her.
Lexi and I dated back when we went to North Limbo.

"Lucy, is it working?" Mr. Nasser asks.

I'm staring directly at Miles with my jaw about an inch from the floor, unable to speak. Miles and Lexi used to date?!

"No, it's not working," Miles confirms after seeing my face.

"Okay, well, let's try it again," Mr. Nasser replies. "Add some more details. Change up what's there."

All right. Here we go again. Waves. Sun. Coconut tanning lotion. Surfboards. Um . . . Colin and Georgia and . . .

Lexi has done some not-so-good things, which is probably
what you have heard about around school, like one serious
thing that got her in big trouble at North Limbo.

Ha! See, I knew it! Of course the rumors are true. Me, a bad judge of character? *Puh-lease.*

"What about this time?" Mr. Nasser asks.

"Nope, not yet," Miles confirms.

"Sorry," I say, realizing I'm supposed to be blocking his thoughts from getting in, not celebrating every time I hear something juicy.

Even something as juicy and delicious as a giant ice cream sundae with rainbow sprinkles.

Yum.

"Let's go again," Mr. Nasser says.

Okay, one more time. Let's do this! Um . . . Colin and ghost lessons. Quicksand. Georgia pulling me down into the quicksand. Wait, no, let's move away from that. Surfing. Waves. Sun.

After she did the thing she did, we got into a big fight and that's why we broke up. So you're not entirely wrong about her.

But you were wrong about me.

So he *was* referring to me choosing Colin over him with the whole "writing people off" comment.

Ugh.

"Lucy, perhaps your choice of location isn't the right one," Mr. Nasser says, this time not even bothering to ask whether it's working. "You might have to dig deeper—find a place with more significance, a stronger tie to you and your history, somewhere from your time down in the World of the Living, perhaps."

Think, Lucy, think.

"If it helps," Miles says, "my Wall is a recording studio. Maybe pick somewhere you've spent a lot of time . . . somewhere you sweat, or somewhere you dreamed of being one day."

All of a sudden, I know instantly what my safe place is.

"Okay, let's try it again," I say confidently. "I got it."

"Miles, let's go again!" Mr. Nasser says.

Floor-to-ceiling mirrors from wall to wall. Gray Marley floors scuffed with the white chalk from golden rocks of rosin. Pale-peach barres attached to stark-white walls. Soft, recessed lighting, and hot air that smells like a combination of sweat and lavender and baby powder. The sound of *The Nutcracker* pas de deux playing in the background.

"Lucy," Mr. Nasser says, "is it working now?"

"It's working," Miles replies with a smirk.

"Bravo! Lucy, bravo! That's really good work," Mr. Nasser says, patting me on the back. "You're quite advanced for your age, you know."

Miles smiles. "It's like you can hardly feel the age difference between us, right, Mr. Nasser?"

Clever, I think, directly at him.

I thought so.

"Okay, well, I think that's enough for our first lesson," Mr. Nasser says. "Lucy, keep practicing your safe space. The more you build into it, the stronger it will be. I'll see you both back here on Thursday afternoon."

With that, he grabs his briefcase and waltzes out of the classroom, leaving the two of us staring at each other.

"So, you and Lexi Landen, huh?"

"I don't really want to talk about it."

"All righty," I reply, trying to sound nonchalant. "Your secret is safe with me." After a moment of silence, I add, "Hey, thanks for the tip about the recording studio. It helped a lot."

"Yeah? So what's your safe space?"

"It's my old ballet studio," I say, a little surprised that I'm actually sharing something that private with him and feeling totally at peace with it.

But he did share his with me, so I suppose fair is fair.

"Oh, yeah," he says, with a little chuckle. "I remember the tutu now," he continues, reminiscing about my crossover outfit. "How come that wasn't your first choice?"

I wonder why I didn't think of the studio first, too. Instead, I thought of the beach—and not even the beach back home where my best friend, Felix, and I used to surf, either, but the beach here in Limbo, where Colin and I had our first tutoring lesson, and where Georgia tried to turn me into a smoothie with her sand-blender trick. And why?

"You know what? I have absolutely no idea why I didn't think of it first. That was really silly of me."

"Well, you came around to it in the end, and that's all that matters."

"I guess so."

"Okay, well, I've gotta go to band practice," Miles says.

"Right, yeah. I've got practice, too. Limbos."

"See ya."

As I watch Miles walk away, a funny feeling deep down in my gut starts to gnaw at me, like when you forget your mother's birthday. How did I think that the beach could be safer or more special to me than the dance studio—the place I literally lived and breathed since the day I was born? I mean, what does that say about me or who I've become here? Don't get me wrong, I love my afterlife in Limbo, but I don't want to forget who I used to be . . .

First I'm writing people off, now I'm writing off lifelong passions?

What's NEXT?!

(Do NOT answer that.)

Just then, Cecily and Oliver come running up to me in the hallway.

"There you are—FINALLY!" Oliver calls out. "Where have you been? We have Limbos in like three minutes, and we have no idea what we're doing for the Spirit Carnival!"

"Yes we do!" I shout back excitedly. "I wanted to surprise you guys—earlier today, I signed the Limbos up for the premier noon spot on Stage A for our first public Limbos performance!"

"OMG we are SO not ready to perform in public yet!" Oliver shouts back.

"I hate to say it, but I think he's right, Lou," Cecily says.

"Then we are going to have to *get* ready!" I insist. "Look, you guys know just as well as I do that Georgia is going to come up with the biggest display of school spirit this event has ever seen, and she's got years of cheerleading training behind her. Maybe, just *maybe,* if we announce our performance first it'll throw Georgia off her game a little. We HAVE to do something amazing, because the *only* way that Georgia and her cheer squad—no offense, Cece—are going to leave this carnival with that Spirit Cup is if they impersonate the Limbos and *steal* it from us!"

"Impersonate us? Honestly, that seems likes a *pretty* complicated plan," Cecily says. "I don't think Georgia could pull something like that off—"

"Duh, she wasn't being serious," Oliver chimes in.

"Right. Oops." Cecily blushes.

"Look," I say, "we can do this! I've got the best VP and secretary a ghost could ever ask for, and I know that the three of us can whip this team into shape. Are you with me?"

"I'm with you!" Cecily cries out.

"Fine, I'm with you, too," Oliver says, begrudgingly. "But I get full costume approval!"

"No sequins," I reply.

"How dare you!" Oliver lobs back. "Ugh, fine. But sparkles are nonnegotiable."

"Deal."

"Deal."

"Now, let's go share the great news with our Limbos!" I call out as Oliver and Cecily follow me into the gym.

Let the games begin.

And may the best ghost win.

(Aka me.)

THE TRUTH BEHIND THE SPIRIT

By Stacy Francis

Once again, it's time to put on your Spirit Hats and revel in the joy of the Limbo Spirit Carnival, a time-honored tradition for both North Limbo and Limbo Central Middle Schools in which we offer our thanks to the town of Limbo while expressing our school spirit—all in an effort to secure the coveted golden Limbo Spirit Cup!

But is it really all just fun and games? Or is there a seedy underbelly of this competition in the name of "school spirit" that rears its ugly head time and time again? For the last five years, the Limbo Spirit Carnival has been the cause of strife, mischief, and even rumored expulsion across North Limbo and Limbo Central campuses as students insist on breaking the rules of the Limbo Spirit Carnival one by one, begging the question: Is it all worth it?

"The teachers think the Limbo Spirit Carnival is this great idea," Allie Kit of Year Two says, "but the truth is that all it does is fuel this crazy rivalry between North Limbo and Limbo Central."

Of course, no one can forget the horror that haunted us here at Limbo Central just two years ago, when three students from North Limbo tampered with the precious Cup inside our own hallowed halls, besmirching it with graffiti and all the fixings of an ice cream sundae.

Or the supposed prank that Limbo Central was planning to pull on North Limbo last year. Thwarted before it could be carried out, it was said to have involved superglue and toilet paper.

"We *live* for the Spirit Carnival," says a source who wishes to remain anonymous. "We're supposed to show our school spirit, right? What better way to do that than to pull the greatest prank of all time?!"

Rumors floating around both schools suggest that this year will be no different. That said, we must ask ourselves, is the Limbo Spirit Carnival truly teaching us about unity and school spirit, or is it actually tearing us apart?

Chapter Three
New Kid on the Block

"Did everyone see the article that Stacy sent around this morning?" Briana asks, sitting down at our table.

It's lunchtime, and the entire cafeteria is gossiping about *The Limbolater*.

"How could we not see it—she blasted it to the whole school," Oliver replies.

"Typical Stacy," Mia says, rolling her eyes. "Desperate to get the scoop on something before someone else does. I mean, it's only Wednesday—the carnival was just announced. Nothing has even happened yet."

"Well, everyone is talking about it," I say. "That Cup prank North Limbo pulled two years ago sounded pretty major."

"The ice cream?" Chloe asks.

"Yeah."

"It was very messy," Briana confirms. "Literally *and* figuratively."

I glance over at Mia, who looks like a sad puppy.

"The article wasn't even that good," I say, trying to cheer her up.

"See?" Trey adds, looking at Mia. "I told you. Stacy is just front-page obsessed—she'll publish anything for the attention."

"You mean, she'll publish anything for attention as long as it isn't written by *me*," Mia adds.

"You're right, it's a total double standard," Trey says. "And she gives herself preferential treatment. But while she's busy writing lame articles that say a whole lot of nothing, you'll be in the wings looking for the real story."

"Really?" she says. "Promise?"

"Promise," he replies.

They are so cute I could puke.

Speaking of cute, I wonder where Colin is . . . I haven't seen him all morning and we didn't end up chatting on the

Tabulator last night. Not to turn into a total and complete gross-out cheese-ball, but . . . I kinda . . . miss him.

Oh, no, I'm turning into one of those girls who can't be without her boyfriend for, like, a minute!

MUST refocus.

"Honestly, Mia, Trey is right," I tell her. "This is your year—I can feel it! And I'll help you any way I can to get an inside scoop."

Just then, Colin walks over with some unknown, long-haired brunette beauty by his side. It's immediately apparent that she's just crossed over, since she's floating off the ground and her state of solidity is about fifteen percent.

"Hi, everyone!" he says. "This is Kai Li. She's new, as you can probably tell. I'll be tutoring her till she gets her footing."

Everyone chuckles.

(Her footing? Get it? You know . . . 'cause she can't walk yet?)

"I mean," Colin stutters, almost nervously, realizing his joke, "you know what I meant."

This? Is the first I'm hearing about a new student, let alone the fact that she's one of his mentees. I wonder when he found out about her . . . and why he didn't tell me? There has to be some kind of explanation—Colin wouldn't just keep this a secret. I'm sure it'll all get cleared up once we have a chance to talk alone.

But seriously, why does Colin have to tutor every single new girl ghost who appears here—do they not have any other tutors in this place?

Suddenly I realize it's been at least a minute since Colin has introduced her, and I've said literally NOTHING.

Well, nothing out loud anyway.

"Hey, Kai, welcome to Limbo Central!" I say, trying to sound upbeat.

Phony much?

"Thanks," she says as she and Colin sit down across from us.

Well, she's *pretending* to sit. Ah, the good old days.

I try to think of something else to say, but my mind is, like, short-circuiting or something. She's just so . . . pretty.

And *her* crossover outfit is normal—a jean skirt, a pair of

Adidas, a T-shirt, and a zip-up hoodie—perfectly girl-next-door casual.

Unlike my Sugar Plum Fairy getup.

After a few minutes of silence, Kai says, "And you are . . . ?"

"Oh, sorry. I'm Lucy," I say, assuming Colin has at least told her that *I* exist, even if he hasn't had a chance to tell me that *she* exists yet.

But she looks at me blankly.

Okay . . . so she has no idea who I am either?

"Lucy . . . Chadwick?" I continue.

"Well, Lucy Chadwick," Kai says, sounding a bit confused, "it's nice to meet you."

I give Colin a look, but he avoids meeting my gaze, and his face whitens like, well, a ghost.

Who got caught with his hand stuck in the cookie jar.

What in the name of all that is ghostly is going on right now?! Did he not tell her he has a girlfriend? Or that said girlfriend is ME?!

The table is so silent all you can hear is the sound of silverware scraping plates.

Okay, time-out: Let's not start freaking out just yet. There HAS to be a totally reasonable explanation for this, even though he doesn't seem to be able to communicate one right now. He's probably feeling so bad that I'm finding out about her this way that his tongue's tied. That must be it. I'm sure he'll tell me as soon as he pulls himself together.

And, in fact, I'm sure if we *had* spoken last night he would have told me all about her. For now, I just need to be calm and collected.

This? Doesn't bother me one bit.

"So, Kai, where are you from?" Cecily asks, trying to fill the silence.

And possibly stop me from saying or doing something dumb.

"I'm from Hawaii, actually," she says. "Maui."

"I hear the surfing there is awesome," Colin says.

Hmph. Looks like someone magically found his voice again.

"Yeah," she confirms, laughing. "I started surfing before I could even stand."

Oh, goodie, she surfs. She's a gorgeous Hawaiian surfing goddess.

Okay, calm down, Emotional Girl. Take a breath.

Or five hundred.

"Lucy surfs, too," Cecily says. "Don't you, Lou?" Then she kicks me gently under the table, because I've apparently gone catatonic.

"Right. Yeah, I do love to surf. But you're probably way better than me. I always wished I had more time for fun stuff like surfing, but I was too busy. I was a pretty serious ballet dancer back home."

I'm not entirely sure what's coming over me, but I can hear myself starting to sound kind of snobby and showy.

"Oh, really?" she replies. "That's cool."

"Yeah . . . I thought Colin might have told you," I say, though once again, I have no idea why.

"It . . . uh . . . hasn't come up," she replies, looking at me strangely.

And . . . it's affirmative.

Colin definitely hasn't mentioned me.

So what? It's been all of like four hours since she got here? She's just died and she's trying to adjust to a whole new afterlife, so obviously Colin has been focusing on the fundamentals with her—and telling her all about his dancer girlfriend isn't fundamental.

I totally get it. It actually makes perfect sense. And I trust Colin completely. He wouldn't do anything to purposely hurt me. I'm sure he's just been dealing with the big things first, trying to keep her calm and relaxed, like he did with me. He's really good at making people feel at ease. And as a tutor, well, that's like part of the job, right?

So why am I going all survival-of-the-fittest on her?

"I've actually done a lot of dancing too," Kai continues, "from hip-hop to traditional hula."

"OMG, I love hula dancing—you HAVE to teach me!" Oliver cries out, and Cecily and I both give him THE LOOK.

Suddenly I start to feel really itchy.

Like I swallowed a wool sweater.

Or a porcupine.

My cool? Is fading fast.

Here's this new girl who's gorgeous and interesting and

clearly talented, and she gets to spend all this time with my adorable boyfriend who didn't even tell her I'm ALIVE.

Or dead.

You know what I mean.

And let's face it, the last time Colin tutored someone new when he had a girlfriend, things didn't go so well for his girl-friend. Now? That girlfriend is ME.

Welcome back, Karma. How was your trip?

I can't believe I'm about to say this, but a part of me can finally understand how Georgia felt when I got here. I didn't know about her, either. Because he didn't tell me. And now I'm acting kind of possessive over Colin around Kai just like Georgia did around me.

On the one hand, we just got together like less than a week ago, and now he's forced to spend all his time with *her*, so it seems only natural that I would be jealous. I mean, this situa-tion is totally unfair. But on the other hand, when I got here, Colin and Georgia had only been together like a month, so it's like history repeating itself . . .

Grrrr. What do we need a new student for anyway? Couldn't she have just gone to North Limbo?

No. Now I'm not only acting like Georgia, I *sound* just like her, too.

Save me.

"So . . . what's this whole Spirit Carnival about?" Kai asks, sipping on her fruit smoothie.

"It's a tradition," Colin says. "We have it every year. North Limbo and Limbo Central both participate with different booths and events and stuff, and the group that gets the most spirit points wins."

"So, what's everyone doing for their booths?" she asks.

"Well, Lucy started a dance club called the Limbos," Oliver blurts out, "so the group is performing for the first time at the carnival."

"Fun," she says.

But I can't tell if she's saying *fun* for real or in a sarcastic way.

"It is fun, but it's also *really* hard work," I point out.

"I get it," Kai says. "If you ask me, you don't know what hard is until you learn how to hula properly. I mean, it's basically like learning how to disconnect your hips from the rest of your body."

"I don't know," I say, defensively. "Moving my hips all over the place was never challenging for me—the hard part was *not* moving them. But that's what ballet technique is all about."

WHAT is my damage?!

"Anyway . . ." Mia interrupts, "getting back to the Spirit Carnival. *The Limbolater*, which is the school newspaper, always does a coffee and donut stand, mostly for the adults. It never wins, but we're too focused on getting the weekly issue out and reporting on the carnival happenings."

"Nice," Kai says. "What about everyone else?"

"Well, most of us are either on the Limbos or on the cheer squad, or both," Cecily tells her.

Suddenly I realize that someone here must have some inside information about Georgia's plans.

"Hey," I say, "who on the squad knows what Georgia has up her sleeve?"

Crickets.

"I haven't heard anything," Briana says.

"Me either," Cecily says. "I would have told you, obviously."

I notice Colin shifting a bit on the bench, like he has ants in his pants.

(At this point? I kinda hope they're the biting kind.)

"So no one here knows what the cheerleaders are doing?" I prod.

At that precise moment—because the afterlife loves me SO much—Georgia and Lexi happen to walk by our table.

"*My* squad," Georgia begins, putting her hands on the table and leaning in as if she's towering over us, "is currently on a need-to-know basis. The few people who need to know, do. I will reveal it to the rest of the squad when the timing is right. Until then, I'd appreciate it if you didn't interrogate them."

Then Georgia glances at Kai.

"Oh, sorry," Georgia says in her fake sweet voice, lifting her hands off the table. "I didn't notice you there. You must be new. I'm Georgia Sinclaire."

"Lexi Landen," Lexi suddenly speaks, and it's the first time I hear her voice. It's deep and scratchy, one of those voices that makes it sound like she suffers from chronic laryngitis.

I guess she *could* have laryngitis, but something tells me this is just how she talks.

"Don't believe all the rumors," Lexi continues, speaking first to Kai, but then giving the rest of us the once-over. "Only *some* of them are true."

Today she's wearing a pair of skinny jeans, Converse, a black-hooded, zip-up sweatshirt, and a black leather jacket. I spot an old, tattered copy of *The Mysteries of Sherlock Holmes* poking out of the pocket of her sweatshirt.

"Hi," Kai says. "I'm Kai Li. I just got here, but I'm guessing you already know that by looking at me. Colin is showing me the ropes."

A sneaky grin stretches across Georgia's face, and I know immediately what she's thinking. And not just because I can read her mind.

(Which I'm completely not supposed to be doing.)

It's payback time.

Payback Time, meet Karma. You two should have a lot to chat about.

"Welcome to Limbo Central, Kai," Georgia says. "Colin is a great tutor. Everyone just loves him! And, of course, anything he can't answer, *we* can."

"That's nice of you," Kai replies. "Thanks."

"In fact," Georgia continues, "how would you like to get together later on after school? We can walk you around town and give you the lay of the land."

You have GOT to be kidding me!

"That would be amazing, thank you!" Kai answers, excited.

"Great, we'll come find you later," Georgia says, smiling.

Lexi just nods coolly, like she can't be bothered to open her mouth.

Then they walk away.

No, prance is more like it. Well, Georgia is definitely prancing. Lexi is too cool to prance.

Briiing! Briiing!

"That's the bell," says Colin. "We should get you to your next class. I'll just go return our trays to the kitchen."

As he heads off, I turn to Kai. "Listen, Kai, I know you've only been here a few hours, but you should know that Georgia and Lexi aren't exactly, um, the most trustworthy people, if you know what I mean."

"They seem perfectly nice to me," Kai says.

"Yeah, well, you don't know the whole story," I tell her. "It's just . . . things aren't always what they seem."

"No, they aren't," she says, looking me straight in the eye. "I think I'd like to decide who I can and can't trust on my own, thanks."

Then she walks off toward the kitchen to meet *my* boyfriend, leaving me alone.

THAT went well.

Later that afternoon, the Limbos are all gathered for practice in the gym, and I can't wait to have our first real rehearsal!

Except that we can't technically rehearse anything yet because we haven't decided what we're performing.

"Okay, okay," I call out, "quiet, please! We really need to decide what type of dance we're going to do for the Carnival because we've only got, like, a week and a half to rehearse! So, I'm going to call out the choices from last time, and raise your hand if you want to vote for that choice. Ready?"

I run through the list of options, and people's hands shoot up like Whack-a-Moles. When we're done, I tell everyone to take a ten-minute break while Cecily, Oliver, and I review the outcome of the vote.

"So, what's the tally?" I ask Cecily.

"It's all over the place," she says. "I think we gave them too many choices."

"So, now what?"

"Now, Ms. Prez," Oliver says, "*you* have to just make a call."

"Are you serious?"

"Dead serious."

"Ha-ha."

"Look," Oliver says, with his no-nonsense attitude, "we need to know what we're doing and we need to know now."

"But I really hate the idea of pulling rank like Georgia does," I say. "You know I wanted the Limbos to be a club where we all make decisions together and no one gets disappointed. That's why I allowed everyone to put a suggestion in the hat last time."

"That's all fine and good," Oliver says, "but that's not how decisions get made, and that's not how real dance companies are run. Someone needs to be in charge, and that someone is you, PREZ."

"But will people be mad if I don't choose what they want?"

"Definitely," Oliver replies. "And then they'll GET OVER IT."

I suddenly start to feel overwhelmed with everything that's going on. First, in my telepathy lessons with Miles, I completely forget about my ballet studio, like I can only remember the Lucy I became when I got here and met Colin. Then Colin shows up at lunch with Kai and I suddenly go all Georgia on her, feeling threatened by her and Colin, her dancing, and even her becoming friends with Georgia and Lexi. And now I have to turn the Limbos into some dictatorship like Georgia's cheer squad because no one in here can make a stupid decision without me?!

"Look, I wasn't going to tell you this until after practice," Oliver goes on, "but I found out what the cheer squad is doing. And it's good."

"You did!" I squeal. "Who told you? What is it?"

"My friend Edward."

"Edward is on the cheer squad?"

"No, he's on the football team. The cheer squad and the football team are doing their event *together*. Georgia is teaching the football players a cheer routine, like, as a joke performance. The players are going to wear their uniforms and everything. It's going to be hilarious."

"Are you serious?" I bark. "So, Georgia's got the whole football team rehearsing a cheer routine?"

"Yup. And you know once word gets out, EVERYONE is going to want to come and see football players make fools out of themselves. I mean, *I* definitely do."

"So . . . she's been rehearsing the *whole* team?" I ask.

"I think so, at least that's what Edward said. But I guess only a few of the cheerleaders know."

"I swear I didn't know anything!" Cecily squeals.

"I know," I say. "But that means that Colin *did* know?"

"Maybe not?" Cecily says, trying to be positive.

"Oh, no, honey, he definitely knows," Oliver says. "Sorry. And there's more."

"There's MORE?!" I cry out.

"She booked Stage B right in the middle of our performance—starting at 12:30."

"Unbelievable!" I shout, loud enough so that all of the Limbos look at me. "Sorry!" I say. "Just give us one more minute. We'll be right with you!"

Oliver puts a hand on my shoulder. "Look, the takeaway here—right now—is that what Georgia has planned is crazy good, so we've GOT to be better. Which means that you have to make a decision PRONTO."

I'm so annoyed I could scream.

But I won't.

"Oliver?" I say.

"Yes?"

"Thanks for whipping me into shape! I know exactly what we're going to do, and I don't care if I do end up turning into a tyrant—we are going to win this Spirit Cup. Georgia may have silly buffoons doing gymnastics, but we've got real talent."

With that, I turn to address my troupe.

"Okay, listen up, everybody! This is our first-ever Limbos performance, and I want people to take us seriously. For this performance we're going contemporary. I could use some volunteers to help me scope out some music, so who's interested?"

Here's the thing: I can't control Colin being an idiot and not telling me about Kai or Georgia's carnival plans. I can't control Georgia having a completely brilliant idea for her event. And I definitely can't control whether or not Kai chooses to be friends with the Wicked Witch of the West and her new crony.

What I can control? Making sure the Limbos dance circles around those ball players.

It's go time.

And a five, six, seven, eight!

THE LIMBO SPIRIT CARNIVAL RULES

RULE #3:

The winner will be determined by
three criteria: the amount of money
the individual event or booth raises, the
presentation quality, and the display of
school spirit and unity. Helping out your
fellow schoolmates is a great way to display
school spirit! After all, a win for your
schoolmates is a win for you!

Chapter Four
No Pressure

"Good morning, Lucy!" Ms. Lyons says, pushing her red, cat-eye glasses up the bridge of her nose with her finger. "Two mornings in one week—to what do we owe this honor?"

"Morning, Ms. Lyons," I say. "I'm not sure, exactly. Ms. Keaner sent me a Holomail asking me to drop by. She said she had something to talk to me about."

"Well, that sounds exciting!" she replies cheerily.

"It could be. Or it could be horrible."

"Pssh! You kids and your imaginations!" Ms. Lyons chuckles. "I'll tell Ms. Keaner you're here."

I have no idea what Ms. Keaner wants to talk to me about, but thinking about all the possibilities has been taking my mind off things with Colin.

T.G.

(Thank Ghostliness.)

The last two days have been SUPER awkward. He's acting really distant with me, and the only explanation I can think of is Kai's arrival. I mean, he hasn't chatted me up on the Tabulator since Monday night. I thought for sure he was going to message me last night to try to explain the whole Kai secret, and that once we talked it would all make sense. But he never did. He totally lied about not knowing what Georgia and her squad are planning for the carnival. And he didn't even tell Kai that I'm his girlfriend! It's so obvious there's something weird going on, and my head keeps spinning in circles trying to figure out what it is.

Jeez. Whoever said having a boyfriend was fun? Was MENTAL.

I've had one for all of like four days now, and I'm exhausted. And confused. Either everyone in a relationship is lying, or Colin and I are doing it WAY wrong.

A few moments later, Ms. Keaner ushers me into her office.

"So, Lucy, how's everything going with Mr. Nasser?" she asks.

"Fine," I say. "I mean, I think fine. I managed to build my Wall on Tuesday. It's still pretty basic, you know, but it's a start."

"That's wonderful!" she replies, smiling. "I'm glad to hear you're doing well, because that's precisely the reason I wanted to talk to you today. Do you remember when Mr. Nasser mentioned the placement exam, and I told you not to worry about that yet?"

"Yes," I reply, starting to get nervous.

"Now, you know that things in Limbo are different from how they were in the World of the Living. Here, we base your placement in school on your ghost levels, not on your age. The Ghost Leveling Placement Exam is an exam that new ghosts take approximately three months after they've crossed over, during which a team of outside administrators test the ghost's supernatural abilities and officially recommend a placement for his or her ghost year. We've recently been informed that this year's team of administrators will be passing through Limbo unexpectedly, and when we told them about you, they recommended it was time to test you."

"Already? I thought you said the test doesn't happen for three months?"

"Generally that's how it works, yes. But there are always exceptions, and it seems you are one of them."

"But . . . what if I'm not ready?"

"These administrators are trained to know exactly when a student is ready—they've been doing this for a long time, Lucy. If they are recommending that you sit for the exam early, I'm sure they know what they are talking about. I know it's a big surprise, and it's a lot to process, but I want you to know I think you're going to do wonderfully."

"And what happens after I get placed in a year?"

"Depending on where you place, we'll adjust your schedule accordingly and make sure you're in the right classes to keep you stimulated and learning things with other students at your level."

"Okay . . . how do I study for the exam?"

"Mr. Nasser is going to help you with that. He'll tell you all about the exam and what to expect when you meet with him later on today for your lesson."

"So when are they coming? When am I going to take the test?"

"A week from tomorrow—the Friday before the carnival."

"That soon?" I screech. "But what about the carnival? The Limbos' performance?"

"Well, dear, unfortunately their trip was a bit impromptu; we only just learned about it. I know it doesn't leave you with much time, but don't worry. This exam is less about studying and more about preparing. Mr. Nasser will explain it all."

Like I have ANY idea what that means.

"Um, okay, well, thanks . . . I guess."

"It's my pleasure, dear," she says, opening her office door to show me out. "Don't be nervous. Be excited!"

"I'll work on that," I say as I head out.

Okay . . . so apparently I'm supposed to be "excited" that they think I'm advanced enough to take this exam early and everything, but . . .

1. Who gets excited to take an exam?! LITERALLY no one.

2. The timing of this thing couldn't be worse! A week from tomorrow? Right before the carnival? I mean, COME ON.

And . . .

3. What if I'm not ready and I totally bomb this test? I'll let everyone down . . .

But no pressure or anything.

Yeah, right.

I mean, how am I going to get the Limbos ready for this performance and study for this placement exam at the same time? In seven days? What do I look like, a superhero?!

Dial 1-866-RED-CAPE for assistance.

By the time Colin and Kai finally arrive at lunch, I've been sitting at our table for twenty minutes, angrily spearing the same pile of pasta with my fork, as if it attempted to jump plate and its punishment is being forced into this never-ending spiral of doom. Where have the two of them been since the lunch bell rang?

I was actually excited to tell Colin about what happened

with Ms. Keaner! Now all I want to do is take this forkful of spaghetti and catapult it at his face.

But I won't, because throwing food at people is wrong.

Even if they are being totally and completely annoying.

"Hey there," Colin says to me as he puts his tray down next to mine. "What's up?"

Even though I'm mad at him, my heart still starts beating like a million times a second when he gets near me.

Ugh.

"Where have you guys been?" I ask, trying to sound casual.

"Long story," Kai says, smiling at Colin.

So now they have inside jokes?

"My locker door wouldn't close," she continues, "and it turned into a disaster—all my books came spewing out like an avalanche."

"Yeah," Colin chimes in. "Something was stuck in the door and it took me, like, ten minutes to get it out. In fact," he says, turning to Kai, "would you like to keep this as a souvenir?"

He hands her a piece of a broken screw.

"I'll cherish it forever," she jokes.

Great, so now he's some kind of Prince Charming rescuing damsels in locker distress?!

Ack. Forget I said that. I refuse to be that annoying, jealous girlfriend.

Okay, starting over.

"Colin's definitely a good person to have around when you're in a tough spot," I say with a smile.

I wonder if she knows I'm his girlfriend yet . . .

"Oh, so he helps all the ladies out of pinches, then, huh?" Kai asks, giving him a smirk.

Stay calm. Deep breaths.

I wait for him to jump in and straighten this out, but he doesn't.

So I do.

"Well, not *all* the ladies, at least, not usually," I say, trying to sound normal and not like anger-fueled smoke is about to burst out of my ears at any moment and launch me up in the air like a rocket. "Mostly me. After all, that's one of the perks of having a boyfriend, isn't it?"

The second the words come tumbling out of my mouth, I regret saying them. No matter how hard I try, I can't help but end up sounding like I've got something to prove to this girl.

And I hate it.

Kai looks up at us, her eyes popping out of their sockets a bit, indicating her complete and total surprise at hearing this information.

I glance at Colin. He's gone all red in the face, but he quickly tries to cover it up.

"Yup, as the girlfriend, Lucy gets first dibs on pinches," he says.

When he calls me his girlfriend, I get goose bumps. Finally, the truth is out! And if he were, like, keeping me a secret, he wouldn't have admitted it, right? I mean, it took a little while for the truth to come out, but he didn't deny it or just stay quiet like he sometimes does. That's got to mean something.

Right?

"So, Kai, how's your second day at Limbo going?" Cecily asks, trying to distract us all from this super-uncomfortable moment.

While Kai answers her, I turn to Colin.

"So . . . *that* was weird. Are you, like, keeping me a secret for some reason?" I say, much more aggressively than I anticipated.

"What? No, I'm not. It just . . . hasn't come up."

"Okay, I guess I can see that, maybe. But you also lied to me yesterday."

"What do you mean? About what?" he replies, defensively.

"About not knowing what Georgia and the squad are doing for the carnival," I tell him.

"That's different—I didn't lie to you. I just didn't tell you." He looks down at his hands. "Look, she just . . . she asked us all to keep it a secret. I was just keeping my word."

"So . . . you'll lie to me in order to keep your word for her?"

"I didn't *lie*," he repeats, more emphatically this time, almost as if *he's* the angry one. "And anyway, you've been keeping some secrets of your own, haven't you?"

"What does *that* mean?" I cry.

"It means, what were you doing alone in a classroom on Tuesday afternoon with Miles Rennert?"

Of course. Well played, Georgia. Well played.

"I wasn't—we weren't alone, really. We were waiting for Mr. Nasser because he's giving me extra lessons. I wanted to tell you all about it, but we didn't talk on Tuesday night and then Kai appeared on Wednesday and we didn't talk that night either. Everything's been so weird. Obviously, Georgia couldn't wait to tell you what she saw when she passed by in the hallway so she could try and drive another wedge between us."

"Oh," he says, once again looking down, playing with the pasta on his plate. "Extra lessons for what?"

"Last week I discovered that I'm telepathic. So Ms. Keaner told Mr. Nasser, and now he's giving me private lessons so I can learn how to build my Wall. And Miles is also telepathic, so Mr. Nasser asked him to help me."

"Wow, telepathic . . . really? That's kind of major, huh?"

"Yeah, kind of. And there's more."

"More? What?"

"Well, apparently they want me to take my Ghost Leveling Placement Exam early. Like, next Friday."

"Jeez, that's *really* early. You've only been here like a month and a half."

"I know."

We sit in silence for a few seconds, but each second feels like days.

ON THE PLANET VENUS!!

"Well," he finally says, "congratulations, I guess."

"Yeah . . . thanks."

By this point, I've been stabbing my fork into my spaghetti so much, my plate looks like a crime scene.

Could this be any more uncomfortable?!

The answer? NO.

His mouth said congratulations, but his heart is definitely not in it. In fact, I've never seen anyone be less happy for someone they supposedly care about.

Rude much?

I try to change the subject because sitting here in this awkward silence is just making me even more annoyed.

"So, Mia, any luck finding some kind of scoop about the carnival this year?" I ask, hopeful.

"Not yet, unfortunately," she replies. "I keep hoping the story of the century will magically reveal itself by some kind of shift in the spirit-time continuum or something."

I laugh.

"Did you figure out what the Limbos are going to do, Lucy?" Kai asks, and I'm taken aback at her interest.

"Actually, yes, I did," I tell her. "But I still need to figure out a way to bring in the school spirit angle. We get judged based on three things, and one of them is school spirit. I'm just not sure how that's going to fit into our serious contemporary dance piece."

"Does your school have, like, a traditional school song?" Kai asks.

"Um, I don't know," I say. "Do we?" I ask the rest of the group.

"Yeah, but it's pretty terrible," Mia says. "*The Limbolater* ran a piece about it once. It's called 'Upon Yonder Hills.'"

"Well," Kai says, "I have this awesome program on my computer that can take any song and, like, re-create it in a different style to make it sound way better. Maybe we can put a jazzy spin on it, and you can use it as your music? That should definitely earn some school spirit points."

"That's actually a really good idea," I say, puzzled by how cool she's being.

Especially after I went all Georgia on her.

"What can I say?" she says. "I've been known to have a few."

Perfect. Now I've insulted her!

"No," I say, "I didn't mean it like that—like I was surprised. I'm sorry, I'm sure you have tons of great ideas."

"Right," she says, sounding unconvinced. "Well, let me know if you want me to show you the program."

"Definitely," I say. "Thank you."

I suddenly see a way to get Kai on my side and away from Georgia and Lexi. And possibly even make this Colin thing slightly less weird. I don't know why I didn't think of it before—it's actually kind of genius. If I'm going to be completely anti-Georgia about this whole Colin and Kai tutoring thing, I've got to commit!

"So . . . " I continue, "seeing as how you're a dancer, too, would you maybe want to join the Limbos and be in the performance?"

All eyes turn toward me.

Relax, people! It's not like I just skinned a cat or something.

"Um, thanks," Kai says, "that's a really nice offer. Can I think about it?"

Not exactly the answer I was hoping for, but I guess it's better than a flat-out NO.

"Sure, I guess."

"It's just," she continues, "Georgia already asked me to help her with the cheer squad event, so I just want to do the right thing."

Of course.

Lucy, 0. Georgia, 5,999,890.

Why is it that no matter what I do, Georgia is always one step ahead of me? I know school spirit is, like, super important in this carnival and I'm supposed to help out my fellow schoolmates or whatever, but this? Is WAR.

"How about you just come to rehearsal today at four and check it out?" I say. "You don't need to commit to anything just yet."

"Cool."

"Cool."

There's no way in afterlife that I'm letting Georgia get

what she wants this time. First she takes my time slot. Then she takes my boyfriend for the carnival booth. And now Kai?

Uh-uh. No way.

The day she gets Kai on her team is the day I cross back over.

I swear on my unbeating heart.

THE LIMBO SPIRIT CARNIVAL RULES

RULE #4:

The point of the Spirit Carnival is to encourage your classmates and neighbors to contribute something positive to your school. If anyone is caught engaging in any behaviors that deliberately go against the spirit of this event, they shall be disqualified from the next year's carnival and suffer any other consequences the administration deems necessary.

Chapter Five
Surf's Up

"Are you nervous?" Cecily asks me as I'm getting ready to go out.

It's finally Friday afternoon, and all I can say is T.G.

This week? Has been RIDIC.

"Nervous about what, exactly?" I reply. "A, the Limbos' performance; B, this scary placement exam I have to take; or C, the fact that tonight is the first time Colin and I will have been alone together since all this weirdness started?"

Cecily scrunches up her nose like she does when she's confused. "When you put it like that . . . I guess, D, all of the above?"

"D, all of the above, is correct! Nigel, open up door number three and show the lady what she's won!"

"Ha-ha," Cecily says. "Come on, be serious."

"Well, Mr. Nasser said the placement exam is really just about exhibiting my abilities for the examiners—whatever they are. It's not a test of my knowledge, like a math exam. It's a test of my supernatural talent. So I should just relax and perform as best I can."

"That sounds good."

"Yeah, but there are still things that I need to work on. Like my Wall, and controlling my emotions, and stuff like that. And it's still scary."

"I'm sure you're going to do great," Cecily says. "I mean, look how far you've come already. You're like a superghost."

There's a slight pause, and then Cecily looks down at her hands and says, "I wish I had half of your abilities."

"I'm sorry," I say, because I don't know how else to respond.

I understand why she feels the way she does. But the thing is, sometimes, I wish I weren't special at all, because then I could just be normal and enjoy school without all this pressure. I guess it's true what they say about the grass always being greener.

"So," Cecily says, "let's talk about this Colin situation."

"Okay," I begin, sitting down on her bed next to her. "Well, we're going to the beach tonight to hang out and talk. It's the first time we'll be alone in about a week."

"Oooh romantic—going back to the place where it all started!"

"Maybe," I say. "I hope so. I want things to work out so badly. It feels like I've been waiting for this FOREVER. But things have just felt so off all week, and it's, like, the first week we've officially been a couple. Isn't that a little strange?"

"Maybe a little," Cecily admits, though I can tell she feels bad about saying so. "But it's hard trying to figure out how to act in the beginning of something new."

"It is?" I say. "I guess that's good to know. It's just . . . I don't know. I don't exactly like the way I feel around him lately—like I'm nervous and unsure of myself, it's almost like I don't think I'm good enough, or something."

"Don't say that, Lou!" Cecily cries, reaching out to hug me. "You're THE BEST. You're *better* than the best!"

"Right," I say, offering a small smile.

"Listen," she begins, seriously. "I get it. You're nervous because this is the first time you've ever had a boyfriend, and you don't really know what to do or how to act. I felt the same way with Parker in the beginning. When I was alone, or we were in school around people, I totally doubted myself. Like, constantly. But when we were alone together, it was totally different. Once you and Colin spend some time together, just the two of you, you'll feel the same way."

"Really?" I say, feeling slightly relieved.

"Yes, really!" she affirms.

"Okay," I reply, but there's still something at the tip of my tongue that I can't keep inside. "I just . . . I can't help thinking that Colin kind of acted this same way when I first got here and he was with Georgia."

"You're *nothing* like Georgia," Cecily says. "Colin really likes you. It's just been a little challenging getting into a new groove. But you'll get there. I promise."

"Thanks. But what if . . . what if we *don't* get there? What if Colin keeps acting weird, and we never find our groove, and he starts liking Kai and dumps me—just like he did to Georgia?"

"Well," Cecily says, fidgeting with the blanket on her bed, "*if* that happens—and it's a big *if*—then I would be very glad to see you rid of Colin, because there's no way I'm going to let my best friend date such an enormous dodo head."

"A *dodo head*?"

"Yup. A dodo head." She nods seriously. "Now for the most important question: What are you going to wear?" Cecily asks, and we both start to laugh.

Ten minutes—and just as many outfits—later, I'm heading down the stairs to meet Colin on the steps of my dorm. He's already waiting when I walk out the door.

"Hey," I say.

"Hey. You look nice."

"Thanks. So do you," I say, and he does. No matter what weirdness is going on between us, I can't deny that Colin always looks SUPER cute. Tonight he's just wearing a pair of jeans and a T-shirt, but I'm still swooning.

Smitten much?

"So . . . tell me about this whole telepathy thing," he says, and we walk toward Death Row and the promenade. "How'd it all go down?"

"Um, well, it started during play rehearsals last week. All of a sudden, I began hearing odd noises, like this faint sound of traffic in my head. After a while, the sounds crystalized and I realized I was actually hearing people's thoughts. Like, from inside their minds. It was so strange."

"I'll bet," he says.

There's a long silence.

Then Colin finally speaks. "You didn't say anything."

"At first I had no idea what it was—I thought I was losing it. And then once I realized, I don't know, I guess I wanted to sort of get control over it first before telling everyone about it."

"Right. So, how did you find out about Miles? Man, I didn't even know he was telepathic."

"We were taking a walk during lunch one day and suddenly I could hear what he was thinking, and even though I kept trying to stop it, I couldn't. I said something about one of the things I heard him think and that tipped him off."

"I didn't realize you guys hung out so much."

"We don't, really. But once he knew that I could read his mind, he told me that he can do it too, and offered to help me. It turns out we can kind of speak to each other, mind to mind."

"So you guys can hear everything we're thinking, and then you can telepathically talk to each other about it?" he says, sort of abrasively.

"That's not exactly how it works," I tell him. "We're not supposed to be listening in, that's why I'm having those extra lessons. So I can learn how to block everyone out."

"Okay . . . well, did you hear any of *my* thoughts?"

Oh, boy, here we go. Again.

"I'm not sure. It was all kind of a jumble," I say, hoping the little white lie will be worth it.

Wash. Rinse. Repeat.

He exhales loudly and smiles. "That's good."

We arrive at the beach and sit down near the rocks where we had our first lesson over a month ago. I don't know how to sit or where to put my hands. Everything feels so . . . off. Should I leave my hands out where he can grab hold of one? But that feels SUPER unnatural. Still, crossing my arms—which is what I really want to do—is definitely not sending the right message.

Hmph.

I settle on crossing my legs—not my arms—and place my hands down in front of me, kind of draped over my knees. Accessible but not totally obvious.

Solid plan.

Colin sits down with his legs stretched out in front of him, toes flopping to the sides, close enough so his thigh is resting just under my right knee, grazing it. It makes me think about the bus ride we took to the beach for our first mentor lesson—how badly I wanted him to hold my hand—even though I knew he wouldn't. That seems like it was a hundred years ago; so much has happened since then. And yet, I'm still sitting here wondering if he'll hold my hand, which is one of those things you shouldn't have to wonder about your own boyfriend, I think.

Even so, I still kind of want him to.

"It's always so nice here," I say, finally, to break the silence.

"Yeah, it's one of my favorite spots, ever since we came here that first time."

My heart starts pounding quickly. Finally things feel like they're getting a little more normal.

"Me too," I say, looking at him.

He looks back at me—straight into my eyes—and I feel like something good is finally about to happen, when all of a sudden a gust of sand blows in our direction and showers us in the face.

"What was *that*?" I wipe my face, spitting sand out of my mouth.

"Oh my god, we're so sorry!" a familiar voice cries out.

Loud giggling follows.

I finally clean enough sand out of my eyes to see Georgia, Lexi, and Kai standing in front of us.

"We were just messing around," Kai says. "We didn't know anyone was behind the rock."

Please tell me the sand has permanently damaged my vision and I'm not really seeing what I'm seeing. WHAT are they doing here?!

"Uh, it's okay," Colin says, flustered.

"Are we, like, interrupting something?" Georgia asks, even though she clearly knows the answer.

Of course Georgia would bring Kai here! I should have known she would stop at nothing to take something this special away from me. I bet she hired a private investigator or something to find out where we were coming tonight just so she could follow us here because she's so—

"I had no idea you guys would be here tonight," Kai says apologetically. "It's just, when Colin brought me here for my first lesson, it was so pretty that I suggested we come here tonight to hang out. It's totally my bad."

So THAT'S what an aneurysm feels like.

"I'm sorry, I think I just blacked out for a second or something—what did you say?" I ask Kai, incredulous.

"Just that after Colin showed this place to me, I really wanted to come back, you know, because, I mean, look at it! He said he thought it was going to remind me of home, and he was so right—it totally reminds me of Hawaii. But I definitely didn't mean to intrude."

When *Colin* brought her here?! So he took her to the same exact spot he took me for our first lesson? That's just perfect. Here I am, thinking this spot is so special—that *tonight* is special. That it's going to be this amazing evening when we rekindle whatever it is I thought we felt for each other that's gotten all messed up this week because of HER, when it's really all just a big fat lie. This spot isn't special at all. Apparently, Colin brings every stinking girl he tutors here!

I suddenly feel incredibly sad. And angry.

I'm *sangry*.

I feel like I could throw a toddler-size tantrum.

But I won't.

Because that's exactly what Georgia wants to see me do right now, and I can't just hand this over to her on a silver platter. She's staring at me with that smirk on her face, just waiting for me to lose it, and I refuse to give her the satisfaction.

I glance over at Colin, who has conveniently turned into Picasso, carefully perfecting his drawing in the sand as if his life depends on it. I glare at him, hoping the heat from my eyes will somehow send electric shocks to his fingers.

It doesn't.

He's too afraid to look back at me.

"Well," I finally say to break the silence, "Colin certainly knows all the best spots around here."

"You guys don't mind if we join you for a bit, do you?"

Georgia pipes in. "We've been running all over this beach. We could really use a breather."

Kai looks at me hesitantly, but Lexi just plops down on the sand by Colin without as much as a glance in our direction. She's fixated on her Tabby as if she's playing the lottery, and hasn't said a word or as much as looked in our direction during this entire exchange.

I wonder what could possibly be so important.

Her book of choice today is *The Wonderful Wizard of Oz*. I can see it spilling out of the back pocket of her cut-off jean shorts.

Georgia walks around to the other side and places herself right next to me, then leans in and whispers, "Not so easy to brush it off when the shoe's on *your* foot, is it Lucy?"

The thing about Georgia is that she can hone right in on the one thing you're most insecure about—and then she beats you over the head with it until you wish you were dead.

And not *alive* dead.

Dead dead.

She may be sad and mean and vengeful, but she enacts her revenge with a level of insight that is truly MINDBLOWING.

And another thing: The girl's always right!

This situation? Is exactly what I told Cecily I was afraid of before I left for this stupid date in the first place! This is the same thing that happened to Georgia when I showed up. I was this pretty new toy, and suddenly Colin was taking me to special places to remind *me* of home, and ignoring his girl-friend, and acting like he was stuck in some relationship he didn't want to be in.

And now he's starting to do the same exact thing to me.

But there's one big difference: Kai might turn into me in this twisted scenario, but I'm NOT going to turn into Georgia. If there's only one thing about this I can control, this is it.

I ignore Georgia and turn my attention to Kai. "You were SO great in Limbos practice, yesterday," I tell her. "Colin, you wouldn't believe how talented this girl is!"

Yes, I admit, it's a bit over the top, but I'm going to dig my way out of this mess and come up smelling like roses.

If it's the last thing I do.

"Thanks, Lucy. But it's still really hard not being able to stand," Kai says. "Once I get back to normal, I'll be so much better."

"Nonsense!" I squeal, smiling. "You're a natural. I can tell already."

Georgia gives me a look so cold it could freeze a small dog.

"In fact," I continue, "I would love it if you would help me choreograph the Limbos' piece for the carnival. I mean, you already have a great idea for the music, which I'm totally going to take you up on, by the way. Maybe I could come by your room later and you can show me the software you were telling me about; that way I'll have the music for tomorrow's rehearsal."

"Sounds great!" Kai says, somewhat bewildered. "Thanks."

Georgia's mouth purses up like she just ate a lemon-flavored Sour Patch Kid.

Victory, thy name is LUCY!

Then, all of a sudden, Lexi's Tabby goes off and she grabs Georgia's arm. "We've got to go, like, now!"

"It's time?" Georgia asks, concerned, then quickly acts like she shouldn't have said anything.

Lexi stands up and pulls Georgia up too, almost by force. Something suspicious is going on. Lexi? Is T.R.O.U.B.L.E. What's it time *for*? Are they planning something? Some kind of . . . prank maybe?! I mean, Lexi's already known to have done something back at North Limbo that got her kicked out of school right around this time of year—even Miles confirmed that. Could that "really bad thing" have had to do with the Spirit Cup prank that Stacy wrote about in that article? Is she up to her bad ways again this year, planning another prank?? If *that's* the case, aren't I under some kind of obligation to let someone know? After all, the whole point of this carnival is to encourage positive school spirit, and pulling pranks doesn't feel very school spirit-y to me . . .

"Kai, you coming?" Georgia says, offering a hand to help her stand up.

Kai takes it.

I want to pull her back down, and scream, "NOT A CHANCE!"

But I can't, because that would be super weird, and my behavior this evening is already pushing it. I rack my brain to figure out a way to warn Kai that she might be getting mixed up in something really bad without everyone hearing, but there are only five of us, and subtlety is not Emotional Girl's friend.

As I watch her walk away, I make one last-ditch effort to bring her over to the good side. "Kai, a bunch of us are going out tomorrow night to hear our friends' band play. You wanna join us?"

"Um, sure!" she calls back, and I feel like not all hope is lost.

Then it's just me and Colin.

We sit there in silence for a few minutes. Normally I'd have so much to say that I wouldn't even know where to begin. But in this moment, after everything that's just happened, I don't want to say anything at all.

"Can we just go back now?" I ask, standing up and brushing the sand off my clothes.

"Yeah," he says. "Sure."

The silence during our walk is deafening, and my ears don't stop ringing the whole way home.

"Come on, Lou, cheer up!" Cecily begs, bringing a mug of hot cocoa over to our table at the Clairvoyance Café and placing it in front of me. "Don't even try to resist smiling—I *know* how much you love chocolate. I live with you, remember?"

She's got a point there. I do love me some chocolate. But not even my favorite candy bar of all time (Twix, duh), can secure a full-fledged smile from me tonight.

It's Saturday night and Figure of Speech is about to perform, so everyone is here to watch, including Kai, who I invited yesterday after what will heretofore be referred to as THE WORST DATE OF ALL TIME.

Kai's approximately forty percent solid now, and the more opaque she gets, the prettier she becomes.

Plus, Georgia is here with Lexi, who looks like she's been dragged kicking and screaming, and is protesting by reading *Wuthering Heights* at the table.

We're just one big, happy family.

"Thanks, Cece," I say, offering a mini smile. Then I bend down to take a sip.

Colin is here too, but things between us are even more awkward than they were pre-date, which is something I didn't think was possible. I find my eyes wandering onto the stage where Miles is, and a serenity falls over me. Everything with Miles is so chill and uncomplicated.

I mean, except for the attitude he pulled on me the other day. But we moved past it pretty quickly, I think.

As the band plays, I can't help but wonder what things would be like if . . . if I *hadn't* chosen Colin. I certainly wouldn't be in this mess right now, worrying about whether he's pushing me out the way he pushed Georgia out because there's a new girl in town who's caught his attention. And I doubt I'd be fighting with Georgia over Kai like four-year-olds dueling over a new doll. I don't think I'd be feeling so rotten about myself, either.

If Miles were sitting here with me instead, I bet we'd be talking about the exam I have coming up, and what we're working on with Mr. Nasser. Maybe how things with the Limbos are going, or his music. Stuff that actually matters.

At that moment, Miles glances at me and we lock eyes. He smiles, then turns back to his keyboard.

Sigh.

In between songs, I decide to do something dumb. I poke the bear.

"So, Georgia," I say, and the whole table turns to stare at me. "Where did you guys run off to in such a rush yesterday when you left the beach? Seemed like something top secret was going down . . . "

Lexi looks up from her book and catches my eye. For a moment I think she's going to speak, but Georgia beats her to it.

"Top secret cheer carnival business." Georgia smiles widely. "Colin knows *all* about it," she continues, then feigns a look of shock. "Oh, but wait, he's keeping that a secret from you, isn't he? Such loyalty—whatever did I do to deserve it?"

Colin shoots Georgia a look, and for a moment I think he's going to actually say something—to stand up for me.

But he doesn't. My entire body deflates.

"So," Mia says, jumping in to try and save the conversation from going to THE BAD PLACE. "Kai, how was your first week at Limbo? Well, not week, I guess. It's only been a few days, right?"

"Three and counting," Kai says, and it takes me back to my first week at Limbo. Three days in, I hit one hundred percent solidity, and I was finally able to do my hair. But I was still stuck in my stupid leotard and tutu. Kai's still sporting her crossover outfit, too.

But as we've already established, she looks adorable in it.

Even if she is still sixty percent see-through.

"It was okay, I guess," Kai continues. "I wish I could get a handle on this whole manipulating matter thing—it's really throwing a wrench in my ability to, you know, do anything."

"You'll get the hang of it eventually," Trey says.

"Colin's a *really* good tutor," Georgia adds, trying to fuel the fire. "I mean, he tutored Lucy when she first got here, and she's, like, super advanced now."

"Lucy's advanced because she's special," Cecily chimes in. "It doesn't have anything to do with Colin."

I give Cecily a small smile.

"All *I* know," Georgia begins, "is that one day Lucy was floating and barely able to hold her own books, and the next she was a hundred percent solid and photographing ghosts like a pro. I guess I just *assumed* it was all of those hours she and Colin spent at the beach together."

"I guess you assumed wrong, like always," I reply.

"Well, I doubt I'm special," Kai says, oblivious to the verbal sparring match Georgia and I are participating in, "and I'd be totally lost without the extra tutoring sessions. I mean,

I wouldn't even be able to sit in this chair if it weren't for Colin! I seriously owe you," she says, looking at him.

"It's nothing," Colin says, finally. "I'm just doing what the school tells me to do."

"Still, if you ever need anything from me, I owe you," Kai replies.

"There is one thing Colin's been talking about that you can definitely help with," Georgia says, and we all shift in our seats, bracing ourselves.

This? Is going WAY overboard.

"He's always wanted to learn how to surf. Haven't you, Colin?"

My face goes beet red, and I have to use all of my strength not to hurl this cup of cocoa across the room.

"I can totally teach you!!" Kai shouts, completely clueless to, well, everything. "Seriously, it's so easy. And it's the least I can do."

Everyone's jaws are practically touching the surface of the table at this point, and Kai finally looks around and realizes something doesn't seem quite right.

"What?" she asks. "Is everything okay?"

Once again, Colin says nothing.

How did things change so drastically in four days?! We just talked about me teaching him how to surf on Monday night—we said we'd do it right after the carnival was over! And now, what? He suddenly has amnesia or something?

I didn't realize I was dating a mute.

"Everything is great," I say, standing up. "Kai, you should totally teach Colin how to surf. Georgia's right—he's been talking about it for ages. I'm sure he'd be delighted to have a skilled teacher like you."

I excuse myself from the table and head toward the front of the room, closer to the band. Right now I need to get away from Georgia, Kai, and Colin before I do or say anything I'll regret.

I'm just going to focus on Miles. Cool, calm, collected, sweet Miles.

"Are you okay?" Cecily says, sidling up behind me. "That was really rough. Georgia is in rare form tonight."

"I'm fine," I say calmly. "I just kind of want to be alone for a few minutes, okay?"

"Sure, Lou. I'll be right over there if you need me."

"Thanks."

I take a few deep breaths and start to think about my safe place. I know I don't really need to work on my Wall right now, but something about it makes me feel immediately, well, protected. I guess that's why it's called a safe place, huh?

Miles's eyes find mine again.

I hold his gaze, and I want to talk to him so badly—I don't even know what I want to say, but I want to say *something*.

Okay, if I'm so powerful, how do I make people disappear? I ask him, with a raise of an eyebrow.

You stop caring what they think.

You really are older and wiser, aren't you?

So you keep telling me.

Miles throws me a wink and then goes back to concentrating on his set.

Even though everything is still a mess—Colin is still being a jerk, Georgia is still being, well, Georgia, and Kai is completely unraveling my life—for some strange reason, I feel incredibly calm right now.

Maybe it's thinking about my safe place.

Maybe it's knowing that someone here understands me.

Whatever it is, I'd like it to never go away, please.

(Thank you.)

"WE INTERRUPT YOUR CLASS TO BRING YOU AN URGENT MESSAGE FROM PRINCIPAL TILLY."

"Attention, attention! This is Principal Tilly with an URGENT announcement! I have just been informed that the Limbo Spirit Cup has been taken from the North Limbo display case. It was present and accounted for on Friday afternoon when school let out, but was first noticed missing Monday at 6:30 A.M. Any student who knows anything at all about this matter should report the information to me at once. Anyone who is found to be involved in the Cup's disappearance will suffer serious consequences. I warned you once about foul play, and I meant it! I will not tolerate this behavior on my campus. If the Cup is not found and returned unharmed, either to myself or to any faculty member at North Limbo, the Spirit Carnival will be canceled."

Chapter Six
The Rumor Mill

I've been counting down the minutes until this very moment all day long, and it's finally here—my next private lesson with Mr. Nasser and Miles. As soon as Ms. Tilly made that announcement this morning, I knew my instincts about Lexi and Georgia were DEAD on.

No pun intended.

I mean, what are the odds that it's just a coincidence? On Friday, Lexi gets this top secret message that sends them bolting from the beach on a mysterious mission, and first thing Monday morning, Ms. Tilly announces that the Cup has gone missing from North Limbo? It couldn't fall more perfectly into place if it were staged!

And *that's* why I can't wait to see Miles. He knows Lexi—like, *really* knows her. I have to get him to talk.

Just then, he enters the classroom.

"Howdy," I say, smiling.

"You seem chipper. What gives?"

"A girl can't be happy for the sake of being happy?"

"Not if the girl is you." He laughs.

"That's lovely."

"Prove me wrong," he says, smirking.

"I can't," I confess. "Fine. I need you to tell me everything you know about Lexi."

"Forget it."

"Come on! It's *really* important."

"And *why* is it important?"

"Because," I whine, "I'm, like, ninety-nine percent sure she's involved in this prank on the Spirit Cup, and as caring students, it's our duty to report any behavior that goes against the spirit of the carnival."

"You're unbelievable."

"Thank you!"

"That wasn't a compliment," he says, rolling his eyes. "Just because I told you she got mixed up with a bad group at North, that doesn't mean everything bad that happens is automatically her fault."

"I know that," I say, "it's just . . . I was with her on Friday afternoon and she got this text message, and right after it she told Georgia they had to go and they, like, ran off on some weird secret mission. I know it doesn't sound like much right now, but you had to be there. There was definitely something suspicious going on. And Principal Tilly did say that the Cup went missing on Friday after school let out."

"Actually, what she *said* was that it was there when school finished on Friday and was discovered missing on Monday— when it went missing is anyone's guess," he replies. "But let me get this straight: Lexi gets a text message and then after she receives it she and Georgia leave your wonderful company, and *that's* your proof that she's involved in this prank?"

"Like I said, I know it doesn't sound like much but . . . just *trust* me, it was suspect."

"Trust you?" he repeats.

"Yes. Don't you . . . *trust* me?"

"Under normal circumstances, yes. But when it comes to Georgia—and now Lexi—I'm not so sure. All reason just flies out the window with you when Georgia is involved."

"Will you at least just tell me if the thing she got kicked out of North for was related to the prank on the Spirit Cup that year?" I beg, and I can tell he's just about to cave when we get interrupted.

Foiled!

"Good afternoon, Ms. Chadwick and Mr. Rennert!" Mr. Nasser sings, making his way into the classroom and slamming his briefcase onto the desk. "Oh, how I love it when my students are prompt! Now, Ms. Chadwick, your placement exam is in exactly four days, so we don't have any time to dillydally. You have exactly one minute to build your Wall before Mr. Rennert here starts reading your precious thoughts."

Okay, I'm getting pretty good at building this thing, but doing it in exactly sixty seconds is advanced, even for me. Is this what they're going to test me on?

"Are you ready?" he continues. "And three, two, one, begin!"

I close my eyes and concentrate as I draw the picture of the studio in my mind. It's almost like a floor combination at this point, with all the pieces of my safe space dancing together to the music until they form this perfectly fluid movement. I'm already picturing myself waltzing across the floor when—

"Really well done, Lucy," Mr. Nasser says, proudly. "You obviously have a great handle on your safe space, and your Wall. Now I want to see if you can break through someone else's, while still keeping yours intact. Do you see a window or a door in your safe place?"

"Yes."

"Excellent. I want you to imagine that if you lift up the window or open the door, that opening can act as a gateway to Miles's safe place."

"Okay."

"I want you to see if you can keep the rest of your Wall intact while you try to break through Miles's Wall. In the meantime, he'll be trying to break through your Wall."

"It sounds very stressful," I confess.

"Perhaps it will be, at first, but once you get the hang of it, it won't feel that way at all. Think of your Wall as an extension of your body. You can move parts of your body independent of one another and still keep them connected, can't you? Well, it's the same basic philosophy with this. Are you ready?"

"I guess."

"Okay, let's go. Three, two, one!"

All righty. I've got my safe place—everything is in order. *Nutcracker* music? Check! Barres and white walls and Marley floors? Check! And there's the window. Okay, let's just gently open it up to let some cool air in.

The breeze feels nice.

I'm climbing through the window now, walking down this narrow passageway that connects my safe place to Miles's. I imagine a door. I try turning the knob but the door is locked.

I don't know what to do. I've never broken into a locked room before.

Lexi probably knows everything there is to know about breaking into locked doors. I wonder if Miles is so protective of her because he still has feelings for her? I wouldn't be surprised. I mean, they would make a ridiculously cool couple.

Yuck. I can't believe I just thought that.

VOM.

What is wrong with me? What's it to me if he does have feelings for her? I mean, it's not like he and I are a thing, or would ever be a thing. And anyway, I still have this whole Colin mess to sort through and—

"Let's stop there for a moment," Mr. Nasser says. "Lucy, you got a little distracted and lost hold of your Wall. Did you feel Miles inside your head?"

"You were in my head?" I screech, giving Miles a shocked look. "No, I'm sorry. I didn't feel anything."

"No need to apologize," he says. "You're still new to all of this. But just know that you need to stay very focused and be careful not to let your mind wander."

FAT CHANCE.

Wait a minute . . . does that mean Miles heard everything I was thinking about him and Lexi?!

Note to self: STOP THINKING ALL THOUGHTS!!!!

After twenty-five more minutes of failing said task, it's time to call it quits.

"Now, Lucy," Mr. Nasser says, "tomorrow we'll meet back here—same time—and we'll work on some other skills for the exam, okay? Miles, you can take tomorrow off."

"Thanks, Mr. Nasser," I say.

He smiles and nods, grabbing his briefcase. Then he heads out of the classroom.

"If you want to work on this some more," Miles says, "I have some time later on. We could meet up. You know, only if you want."

"That would actually be really great," I say, smiling. "Thanks."

"No problem," he says, heading for the door. "How about seven o'clock in the library?"

"Works for me."

"Oh, and one other thing," he calls out.

"What's that?"

"I don't."

"You don't what?"

"Still have feelings for her," he offers, with a sly smile. "See ya later!"

I guess I should have known that whenever we're in Mr. Nasser's classroom, all thoughts are fair game, right?

I sprint off to find Mia to report my prank theory and spot her coming out of *The Limbolater* layout room.

"Mia! Mia!" I cry out, and she turns around and heads my way.

"Hey, girl, what's up?" she says.

"Have I got a scoop for *you*!"

"'Bout what?"

"The Cup prank!" I squeal.

"Are you serious? Dish it now!"

I tell Mia all about the text message on the beach and Lexi and Georgia's strange behavior afterward, and the fact that I *know* Miles was just about to crack and fess up to Lexi being involved with that infamous prank two years ago.

"That's it?" she says, unfazed.

"What do you mean, 'that's it'? That's a lot!"

"It's not real evidence," Mia replies. "It's all speculation and hearsay."

"Are YOU hearing what I'M saying?!" I cry out. "This is

your chance! I'm telling you—THIS? Is your front-page article!"

"Okay, okay, maybe there are some good leads here. I'll look into them, all right? I promise."

"Good," I say, smiling. "Now I have to get to Limbos practice! I'm totally late!!"

"Good luck! And Lou?"

"Yeah?"

"Thanks."

At seven o'clock, I meet Miles in the library to work on breaking down his Wall some more, but the truth is, I'm exhausted and my brain feels like scrambled eggs. I really, really, *really* don't want to even think about Walls, let alone build or destroy any.

EVER AGAIN.

What I *do* want to do? Is ask Miles why he told me what he told me about his feelings for Lexi (or lack thereof) after class earlier. But if I ask him *why* he told me that, it'll mean that I care. And if I *care*, that means that maybe I like Miles more than I'm admitting to, and at this point I'm still technically with Colin, even though we haven't spoken more than two words to each other since Friday night.

Which, between you and me? I TOTALLY can't believe. I really thought he would have apologized to me by now, but so far all I've heard is crickets. I'm starting to question what I was thinking, jumping into this relationship thing so quickly. I basically feel like I'm on one of those horrible scrambler rides at the amusement park 24/7, and every hour something else happens that hurls me sideways and makes me regret the last meal I ate.

Tasty.

"What's up?" Miles says, appearing by my side as if out of nowhere.

"Jeez, sneak up on a girl, why don't you?" I joke.

"I have, apparently. So, shall we?"

"Do we have to?" I beg. "My brain feels like it's been blended into a smoothie."

"Ouch."

"Yup. Can we just . . . like, chill for a bit?"

"Sure, I guess."

"You're a bit more talkative than usual lately," I say. "And a bit . . . snippier. There a reason for that?"

"Maybe," he says.

"Would you care to share it with me?" I press.

"Honestly? Before, I guess I was a little bit nervous around you."

"*You* were nervous around *me*?!" I cry out, incredulous.

"Yes. So I was always a little on the quiet side with you."

"And now . . . you're not?" I ask.

"Nope. Not anymore. Because I realized something. Something important. Something afterlife-changing."

"Oh, yeah, and what's that?"

"That at any given moment, you have absolutely no idea what you're doing."

At that, I burst out laughing, and Miles joins me until we're so loud that the librarian storms over in a huff and *shushes* us so forcefully that little bubbles of spit fly out of her mouth.

This just makes us laugh even louder.

Before the librarian can spit at us again, we gather our

books and launch ourselves out the library door, almost hyper-ventilating from the hysteria.

Just then, I notice shadows running across the campus's back courtyard.

Two shadows, to be exact. Each sporting a messy wave of long, ponytail-swept hair.

"Did you see that?" I ask Miles, grabbing his jacket arm and pulling him down into the bush by the side of the library entrance.

"What?"

"Those two shadows," I whisper, "they just ran across the lawn. Look, they're hiding over there!"

"Oh, yeah. That's weird."

"They're carrying something . . . look! It really looks like . . . like a trophy or a . . . Cup! Doesn't it?"

"I mean, I guess, kind of," he replies. "It's really hard to see in the dark."

"Look . . . over there!" I say, pointing to the left of the other two shadows. "There's a third person . . . more long hair, too."

"What? How can you tell?"

"Because the ponytails form a shadow on the ground. They should have worn hats or something. Quick—give me your Tabby. I want to take a picture and send it to Mia!"

"Fine, here. But I'm leaving this bush now," he says, starting to stand up.

"No! Where are you going?!" I cry out, yanking him back down. "This is a top secret fact-finding mission we're on. Those three students executed the Spirit Cup prank—and I'll bet you a million bucks those three ponytails belong to Georgia, Lexi, and Kai. Just wait till Mia gets my Holomail—she's gonna flip!"

"But you have absolutely no proof that it's them," he says.

"Hey, I thought you said you didn't have feelings for Lexi anymore?" I reply.

"I don't."

"Well, if you don't have feelings for her, then why do you insist on protecting her when it's so obvious she's involved?"

"It's not obvious to anyone but you," he replies, seriously. Then he stands up and brushes some dirt off his pants. "Look, I *know* Lexi, and I really don't think she would have anything to do with this. Now it's time for *you* to trust *me*."

I know I'm supposed to say okay and let it go.

But I just can't.

There's that itching inside my gut again that's telling me whatever is going on here *definitely* involves one Destiny's Child–style trio.

"I'm sorry," I finally eke out, "it's just . . . "

Miles looks down. "I'm gonna go home now."

"Miles, wait," I call out after him. "What's the matter? Why are you getting so bent out of shape about this?"

"I'm not bent out of shape, Lucy," he says, calmly. "I'm just over this whole Georgia-Colin-Lucy triangle. Call me if you ever get over it too."

I feel unsettled watching Miles walk away from me. Maybe he's right about this whole triangle thing. Maybe I'm obsessing over this because I'm annoyed with Colin and I'm jealous of Kai and I really, really, really want to stick it to Georgia.

But it's also true that deep down inside, I just *know* it's the three of them.

And now it's time to prove it.

*　　*　　*

Later on that night, I head over to Mia's room to tell her all about what happened in the courtyard.

"Are you sure it was them?" Mia asks, a look of awe on her face.

"I mean, it was dark out so I didn't see their faces in the light," I reply, sitting up on her bed, "but I'm like ninety-nine percent sure. It had to be! There were three of them. They all had long ponytails, and they were definitely holding something suspiciously Cup-shaped. After everything we know about Lexi and the text message, how could we be wrong?"

"It sounds pretty foolproof," Mia agrees. "And the pictures you sent me were decent—the shapes do fit their descriptions. Plus, while you were chasing bandits, I was digging up dirt on Lexi."

"Ooh, did you find anything?" I ask excitedly.

"You could say that," Mia replies, smiling slyly. "I just happened to come across a *Limbolater* dating back to a few weeks *after* the Spirit Carnival, during Lexi's first semester at North Limbo . . . "

"AND?"

"And . . . it claims that one Lexi Landen WAS in fact involved in defacing the Spirit Cup at Limbo Central that year!"

"Are you serious?" I screech.

"Dead serious."

Mia and I spend the next ten minutes squealing and jumping up and down on her bed like we're sugar high off a bag of Halloween candy. Finally, Ms. Sotherby knocks on Mia's door and forces us to say good night.

But I can't stop smiling all the way down the hall.

I'm just gonna go ahead and say it.

I WAS RIGHT!!!!!

I knew the pieces all fit together somehow. Lexi getting kicked out of school right after the carnival her first year. The mysterious text message at the beach. The Cup going missing right afterward. And three ponytail-clad shadows running through the courtyard at night carrying something perfectly Cup-shaped?

This case? Is open and shut.

And now Mia finally has all the facts she needs to make this the best scoop *The Limbolater* front page has ever seen.

And THAT, Stacy Francis, is on the record!

Breaking News from The Limbolater...

THE CUP CROOK STRIKES AGAIN

By Mia Bennett

Two years ago, Limbo Central Middle School was the stage for a cruel and messy attack. These callous Cup crooks broke into our school, took what was ours, and made us the laughingstock of the Spirit Carnival.

And now they're back to do it AGAIN.

According to an inside source, not only is this missing Cup part of a days-long planned heist—the heist in question was orchestrated by at least one of the same members of the original Ice Cream Cup Caper team!

Last evening around 7:30 P.M., three black-clad ghosts with long ponytails and guilty consciences ran across the back courtyard of Limbo Central with the Spirit Cup in hand, preparing to frame our fair school for a Cup crime we simply didn't commit. The source, who not only witnessed the crime firsthand, but was quick enough to snap a photo of the culprits in question, had this to say: "Even though it was dark outside, I could swear that the figure holding the Cup bore a striking resemblance to third-year student Lexi Landen."

After launching a full investigation, *The Limbolater* can in fact confirm that Lexi Landen was involved in the

Ice Cream Cup prank her first year at North Limbo, where she was a student until her unexpected and unexplained leave from the school a few weeks after said incident. Could her illegal sundae be the reason she was forced to exit her previous school prematurely? My sources say yes.

Lexi Landen subsequently enrolled in Limbo Central for her second semester of Year One, where she's still enrolled. Innocent until proven guilty is our motto at *The Limbolater*, and yet, one can't help but wonder if history is repeating itself.

As for the other two ghosts in question? The jury is still out on them, but we have confirmed they were indeed both female, so be on the lookout for a fearsome threesome!

Chapter Seven
Caper Crazy

"I can't get over how amazing that article was!" I whisper to Mia in the middle of our first-period Famous Apparitions class on Wednesday morning.

"You really think so?" she whispers back.

"Yes. It was so professional. And *way* better than Stacy's."

"You're not just saying that because you're my friend, are you?" she begs.

"No way, I would never. It was *really* good."

"Thanks," she replies. "Well, I spent forty-five minutes in Principal Tilly's office this morning going over every single detail that I uncovered and put in that article—so it better be worth it."

"Yikes."

"Ladies," Ms. Roslyn calls out, "is there something you'd like to share with the class?"

"No, sorry, Ms. Roslyn," we both chime in unison.

"All right, then, please be quiet and pay attention. Now, where was I? Oh, yes, from ancient Egypt, to Athens, Greece, ghost apparitions have always been a part of the World of the Living . . . "

I can't concentrate. I'm so excited for Mia I can hardly think. And if there is a subject that could actually keep my attention at this point, it isn't ancient Egypt.

No offense, Ms. Roslyn.

Anyway, Mia *really* deserves this feature. She's worked so hard for the last year and a half trying to get Stacy to give her the front-page beat, and she keeps getting shot down, so this? Is a MAJOR win. Now, if I could just get the rest of my afterlife to head in the same direction . . .

Update? Colin *finally* called me last night when I got home from the library, after days of not speaking. He apologized for bringing Kai to the beach and swore on his own grave that it meant nothing.

His exact words?

"It meant nothing—I promise! I needed a place to take her, and the beach worked so well for you, and she was from Hawaii, so I just defaulted. It was special with you. With you, I planned it."

I guess that should make me feel better, maybe? But it doesn't. The whole situation leaves me feeling . . . uneasy, like I left the house for school but can't remember if I turned the flatiron off.

Will I burn the house down . . . or won't I? That is the question.

It's just . . . I get the sneaking suspicion that relationships aren't *supposed* to feel like this. I mean, don't get me wrong— I've never actually been in one, so this is all based on guesswork. (And really cheesy romantic comedies.) But aren't boyfriends supposed to make you feel, well, happy? And comfortable? And isn't the whole point of the boyfriend-girlfriend scenario that you don't have to wonder anymore whether the other person is into someone else?

Duh.

I'm so confused. I don't want to do anything rash, but I also don't want to keep feeling like this . . .

"WE INTERRUPT YOUR CLASS TO BRING YOU AN URGENT MESSAGE FROM PRINCIPAL TILLY."

"Quiet, everyone!" Ms. Roslyn calls out, and a hush falls over the classroom.

"Good morning, Limbo Central. This is Principal Tilly. I'm pleased to inform you that I've just received word that the Spirit Cup has been returned—unharmed—to its rightful holders, North Limbo Middle School. It was apparently discovered early this morning and has been sent for cleaning and secure keeping until the carnival. Although the Cup has been returned, please know that we are still taking this matter very seriously. We intend to find the culprits of this prank, and when we do, we shall deal with them accordingly. Once again, anyone with any knowledge of this incident should report it to me at once. Thank you, and have a good day!"

I immediately turn to Mia, who looks sadder than a kid with a broken leg at an ice rink.

"I'm sorry," I mouth.

She just raises her eyebrow.

"It's not for nothing, though," I continue, "I mean, she's still looking for the people involved—the article still counts."

"Sure," she says, deflated. "I guess that was my fifteen minutes of fame. Stacy is never gonna let me see the front-page beat again."

Ms. Roslyn spends the next ten minutes trying to quiet us all down, and by the time she does, the bell rings and it's time to go to our next period.

The moment Mia and I exit the room, we're accosted by Lexi and Georgia.

"Uh-oh," I whisper out of the side of my mouth. "Here we go . . . "

"I can't believe you published that garbage," Georgia spits out angrily. "I mean, I know that Lucy is dead set on dragging our names through the mud, but I expected more from you, Mia. I thought we had buried the hatchet."

"That's rich considering how you've been acting," Mia replies. "You completely blew off the sleepover party, and you've been ignoring me and the rest of us all week, ever since you started hanging out with Lexi. But that's beside the point. I wrote the article because I'm a reporter, and that's what I do. I'm not taking sides, but I'm also not here to protect people."

"Not taking sides?" Georgia yells back. "You've had Lucy breathing lies in your ear for the last week and then you write *this*? This has *her* written all over it."

She pauses to glare at me for dramatic effect.

"I did my own research," Mia replies, though I can tell she's getting a little nervous. "I did have a source, but all journalists use sources. And I believe my source."

"Oh, yeah?" Georgia says defensively. "Well, your *source* has a nasty case of Rejection Fever, and she's taking out all her anger over Colin's new girl crush on us. So I'd get a more reliable source, if I were you."

My heart sinks so fast I feel it falling through my stomach, like a spilled can of paint.

It's like I said earlier: Georgia's radar for insecurities is basically CIA-issued.

At this point, Lexi puts her arm out in front of Georgia and steps forward. "Look, you can report all you want, as long as you get your facts straight. Isn't that the first rule of journalism? You might want to go back through that article and have it fact-checked. Come on, G, let's go."

With that, the two queen bees turn around and walk away, leaving Mia with several stings that appear to be swelling by the second.

If only the two of them would drop dead like normal bees do after an attack.

No pun intended.

"Are you okay?" I ask her, putting my arm around her shoulder.

"Lucy, did you *really* see them last night? Or did you just want it to be them so badly that you embellished the truth?"

Okay, this feeling? Is WAY worse than the unsettled feeling I get when I realize I left the house and forgot to turn the flatiron off.

Questions start flooding my mind. Did I want it to be them so badly that I lied? Did I put Mia's job with *The Limbolater* in jeopardy, not to mention our friendship? AM I COMPLETELY AND SOCIALLY WITHOUT A CONSCIENCE?!

But I did see them. I *know* it was them. And I wouldn't make that up.

"Mia, I promise I wouldn't tell you something I didn't believe just to get them in trouble. I would never do that to you."

"I know," she says. "But just because you believe it's true, doesn't make it true. You're so biased when it comes to Georgia, maybe you just convinced yourself it was them because you wanted it to be?"

"I mean . . . I guess that's possible," I reply, thinking back to what Miles said in the library Monday night. "But, I just, really don't think I would do that."

"Maybe you're not as in control of yourself as you think you are," Mia says. "Anyway, it's not your fault. I should have known better. I wanted to get that front-page beat so badly that I would have stopped at nothing to get it. And in the process, I undermined my own journalistic integrity. I should have spent more time fact-checking. I should have researched it more and gotten another source."

"I'm sorry," I say.

Because I don't know what else I *can* say.

Limbos practice this afternoon drags on like a funeral.

Pun intended.

I should be so happy right now. The Limbos are making their performance debut in three days, I have a boyfriend for the first time in my life AND afterlife (at least, I think I still do), and I'm about to get officially placed in my ghost year— any ghost would die for this list of goods!

LITERALLY.

And yet . . . I'm completely and totally miserable. And I can't get Georgia's voice out of my head.

"Let's take it from the top!" Oliver calls out, and I snap back to attention.

"Yeah, let's go from the part in the center with Kai—are you ready?" I ask her, and she nods. "Okay, and a five, six, seven, eight!"

Kai swivels left when she should be going right, and the rest of the trio in the center formation is completely thrown off.

For the tenth time.

I suppose I can't really blame her. She's still fifty percent see-through and she can't actually keep her feet on the ground yet.

Still, we don't have any more time for excuses.

"Kai, you went the wrong way again!" I cry out, frustrated. "Let's try it one more time."

"But wait," Kai squeaks, "can I just—"

"I'm sorry," I interrupt, "we don't really have time to debate it right now. The performance is in three days, so we need to get this sequence right. Let's take it from the top of the section!"

Oliver and Cecily throw me a look, but I pretend not to see it.

Fine, I know my reaction was a little harsh, but we're down to the wire! And Oliver said it himself: Someone's got to be in charge here. And that someone? Is me. And I must say, my cracking the whip Oliver-style is the reason the Limbos are looking pretty good right about now.

At least they would be, if it weren't for Kai.

I never should have included her in this. She's not ready. She can barely stand on her own two feet, for crying out loud! But did I think about that? No. I just *had* to invite her to join the group. And then I just *had* to ask her to help me choreograph, didn't I?

What in Limbo was I thinking?!

I'll tell you what I was thinking: I was thinking that I could finally show Georgia that I can win. Just once. That I could get Kai to like me better, and then we'd become best friends and she wouldn't be a threat to me and Colin. I was jealous and selfish, and winning was all that mattered to me.

That's what I was thinking.

You know what else I *didn't* think about? The other Limbos members and how hard they've worked for this day that I am totally and completely decimating with all of my bad choices.

Georgia was right. I am suffering from Rejection Fever. It's creeping its way through my bloodstream (or it would if I had blood) and slowly making it impossible for me to think straight! I mean, why am I going out of my way to be so nice to this girl anyway? It's the members of the Limbos whose feelings I should be worrying about—not Kai's. I should have my eyes on the prize, and that's the Limbo Spirit Cup.

"Stop!" Oliver cries out. "Kai, you did it again."

"I know," Kai calls out. "If I could just make a small adjustment to the choreography, then—"

"Enough!" I cry out, before I know what's hit me. "Kai, I'm sorry, but I just don't think you're advanced enough for this part. We'll have to give you something different. Allie—you can sub in for Kai this time."

The whole Limbos team looks at me in shock.

"Ready?" I continue. "From the beginning."

Kai steps out of position and comes marching up to me. "What's that about? I thought you said I was super talented— so talented you wanted me to help you choreograph! But every time I suggest anything you go mental, and now you're even taking away my part?"

"You're right," I say, because I'm so tired of pretending. Even if telling the truth makes me a monster. "You're right. I said all of those things, but I didn't actually mean any of them. I was just jealous of you spending time with Colin, and Georgia was egging me on, so I invited you to join the Limbos and I asked you to help me so you would be on my side."

"On *your* side?" Kai looks disgusted.

I feel myself turn three shades of embarrassed.

"Yes. It's awful, and I'm sorry," I reply. "But I'm just being honest. You don't understand what Georgia is like. She completely gets under your skin like a parasite and then slowly eats away at your insides until you have nothing left."

Whoa, that got gross pretty fast.

"So because Georgia's a pill, that makes it okay for you to be equally rotten?" Kai says.

"I didn't mean that," I say, trying to backtrack. "I'm just . . . I'm just trying to make you understand where I'm coming from in all this."

"Don't bother," Kai says. "I know everything I need to know already. You can save the *tips* for your next article." Then she storms out of the gym.

Ugh.

If I don't figure out a way to turn this story around, the next article I'll end up in is the crime blotter.

DOA.

(Dead on arrival.)

Just as nature intended.

The Limbo Spirit Carnival Rules

Rule #5:

Every carnival group-sponsored event must designate a group leader who shall be present on the booth or event grounds throughout the entirety of the event. This person shall be in charge of their group's earnings and shall report these earnings to the carnival committee using the honor code.

Chapter Eight
Just Kidding

The judgment day has come at last . . .

You know, my placement exam? Yup. It's Friday morning, and I'm on my way to Ms. Keaner's office right now.

I'm SO nervous, but I can't concentrate AT ALL. I know I should be laser-focused, but all I can think about is Georgia and Lexi and Kai, and how bad I feel about the fight Kai and I had the other day. I *wanted* to apologize to her yesterday, but I couldn't.

BECAUSE SHE WASN'T HERE!

All day yesterday, the three divas were mysteriously missing from school grounds. My guess is that it had something to do with the disappearing Cup, and by the looks of all the whispering in the hallway this morning, everyone else thinks so, too.

Perhaps I wasn't so wrong about that whole scenario after all—not that that's at all what I'm supposed to be thinking about right now. It's just . . . if I wasn't right, and I didn't actually see them the other night outside the library, then what could possibly be the reason for all three of them being absent from school yesterday? On the other hand, if they *were* innocent, maybe Principal Tilly gave them all some kind of day off due to the fact that we wrongfully incriminated them in the school newspaper and blasted it to the entire school?

Oops.

Okay, never mind all of that. Right now, I HAVE to concentrate. I'm sitting for this placement exam in less than twenty minutes and I need to be completely and totally calm.

Emotional Girl is NOT invited to partake, thank you very much.

"Good morning, Lucy," Ms. Lyons croons as I walk through the door to the administration office.

"Morning," I reply, taking a seat to wait for Ms. Keaner.

By this point, I totally know the drill.

I pick up a copy of *HEALTH & SHAPEshifting* and start scanning the main article, "Shapeshifting into a Happier You!" about a detective ghost who shapeshifted into a yoga instructor to catch a crook, and how it changed her whole afterlife.

I wish I could shapeshift into a happier me right now, but Emotional Girl has dibs. I can't stop thinking about that look on Kai's face when I said what I said the other day. I didn't mean to be cruel—I was just trying to be honest! When Georgia gets under my skin, I literally can't help myself. I lose it and go to the crazy place. But for some reason, when *she* goes to the crazy place, she manages to get away with it—and apparently it doesn't keep her up at night, either. When I go there, I just feel . . . well, rotten. Why *is* that? I mean, I guess that's a good thing, in a way. If I didn't feel rotten, that would be way worse, right?

I honestly don't know how to fix this.

What I *do* know? Is that I don't like the way I've been acting this week. And I don't like the way I've been feeling, either. It's like I've somehow lost . . . myself. It started with forgetting about my dance studio when I was choosing my safe place, and it's just gotten worse from there. Kai's appearance suddenly turned me into a total fake, and my boyfriend, who's supposed to be helping me figure this stuff out and feel better about everything, has turned into the sour cherry on this spoiled cake.

Mmm . . . delish!

"Lucy, dear!" Ms. Keaner calls out, emerging from her office in a panic. "I have terrible news—the examiners have been delayed on some kind of emergency matter, so I'm afraid you won't be able to sit for your exam today after all."

A wave of relief rushes over me.

"Oh, really?" I say, trying to sound upset. "What happened?"

"I don't know, exactly. All I know is that they won't be arriving here till tomorrow and they are only staying for one day."

"Okay . . ."

"Which means," Ms. Keaner continues, "that I'm afraid you'll have to sit for the exam tomorrow morning."

"Wait, you mean I'll miss the carnival?" I cry.

"I'm so sorry, Lucy. You won't miss everything! But they won't be getting here till around ten, so you'll sit for the exam at ten-thirty. I'm sorry to say that it will certainly cut into the beginning of the carnival events."

"The Limbos' performance is at noon," I reply, distraught.

"The test almost always takes about two hours to complete," Ms. Keaner says apologetically. "Lucy, dear, I'm so very sorry. I know how much you were looking forward to the Limbos' performance. Perhaps we could ask Principal Tilly to move it to another time later on in the day?"

"That wouldn't be fair to the rest of the Limbos," I say. "Noon is the best time slot. It's early enough that everyone is happy and excited, and right before lunch, so people aren't too busy stuffing their faces to come watch. Plus, afterward, the Limbos can just relax and enjoy the rest of the carnival instead of spending the whole day being nervous!"

"With reasoning like that, how can I argue?" Ms. Keaner says, offering a smile. "Listen, I know this is very disappointing, but I promise you that this exam will make everything worth it. It's about your future, after all, and what could be more important than that?"

"Right."

"Now, go off to class and I'll arrange everything for tomorrow. Come back here at quarter to eleven, okay?"

"Sure thing," I say. "Thanks, Ms. Keaner."

"Chin up, Lucy!"

Well *that's* just great. Let's run down the awesome items on today's afterlife menu, shall we?

Breakfast consists of one exam cancellation and one inability to partake in the Limbos' performance. For lunch, the first course is one horribly itchy feeling in my stomach, followed by falsely accusing three people of theft. And finally, for dessert—an assortment of weird fights with boys (i.e., Colin and Miles).

I'd like a word with the chef, please!

Okay, the only *good* thing about the exam being rescheduled? Maybe I can actually right some of these wrongs before I have to do this all over again tomorrow. Because next time? I REALLY need to have Emotional Girl under control.

*   *   *

The first thing I do the second the lunch bell dings is find Kai, who's standing next to Colin by her locker.

"Hey," I say, awkwardly, to both of them.

"Hey," Colin says back, offering a smile. I can see the dimple on his left cheek emerge, and I get little butterflies.

Still, I must not be distracted by silly things like cute faces.

"Kai, can I please talk to you for a minute, *alone*?"

"I'll just head over to the cafeteria," Colin says. "See you in there."

"What is it?" Kai asks, not in full-fledged shutdown mode yet, but not particularly cheerful either.

"I was worried about you guys yesterday," I say. "Is everything okay?"

"*You* were worried?" she says in disbelief.

"Yes, I was worried," I repeat. "Look, I know that you know I'm the reason Mia wrote that article—that *I'm* her source—and the truth is that I still believe I saw the three of you outside the library that night with the Cup. If you tell me right now to my face that I was wrong, I'll accept it. But that night, in that moment, I really believed I was telling the truth. And I still do."

"You mean to tell me that you had no ulterior motive other than to tell the truth?" she asks.

"I wouldn't exactly call it an ulterior motive, but there might have been a . . . bonus," I confess. "Georgia and me? We've got baggage. Lots and lots of baggage. Smack-an-XXL-sticker-on-it-and-charge-us-extra kind of baggage. And she's the *queen* of ulterior motives. She always manages to get away with it, too. You wouldn't believe the stories I could tell you about things she's done. So, this time, I'll admit—I really, really wanted her to get caught in the act. But no matter how badly I'd like to see Georgia get what's coming to her, I would never have put Mia in that position if I didn't feel confident about what I saw."

Kai just stands there staring at me.

"I *am* sorry if what I said got you guys in trouble, though," I continue. "Is that why you weren't in school yesterday?" I ask again.

"Yes," she says. "Thanks to you and Mia, we got taken out of school for questioning, but everything is fine now. And you were right. It *was* us on the lawn. But it's not what you think."

"What happened?"

"The infamous text that Lexi got on the beach? It was from some old friends of hers back at North. *They* were the ones who stole the Cup from their own school and were planning to frame some kids at Limbo Central. Lexi was pretending she was in on it, and then when she discovered where they'd hidden the Cup, the three of us went to get it. We returned it to North on Wednesday morning."

Oh. My. Ghost. I got things SO twisted.

"I . . . I don't even know what to say," I stutter. "I'm so sorry. This is all my fault. Miles was right. I should have just listened to him. He told me he knew Lexi, and he knew she wouldn't get mixed up in something like this. I just wanted to be right so badly."

"Well, you were a little bit right," Kai offers.

"Thanks, that's sweet of you. But instead of obsessing over the one small thing I got right, if I had just trusted my friend, I would have seen all the ways I was wrong. I'm really sorry, okay?"

After a few moments, Kai says, "Okay. But it doesn't make up for how you treated me at Limbos practice the other day."

"I know," I reply, lowering my head, ready for round two. "I'm sorry for that, too. But what I said the other day was true. I wasn't being fair to you when I asked you to join the Limbos before, or when I asked you to help me choreograph—I just said those things to try and win you from Georgia, which I know sounds really lame and wrong. I should have just been friendly to you because you're new, and when I was new, I was really happy to have a friend in Cecily. I'm so sorry. Will you please forgive me?"

"Yes, I'll forgive you," Kai says, smiling. "But only if you don't make me go back to my old part in the Limbos? You were right—I'm so not ready for that yet. Being a ghost is way harder than I thought it would be."

"Deal! Oh, wait—the Limbos! I need to find Oliver and Cecily now. We'll talk more later at practice, okay?"

I dash off to find Cecily and Oliver to break the news to them about tomorrow's Limbos performance, feeling strangely energized. At least I have things with Kai sorted out, but I still have to apologize to Lexi.

And Georgia.

The thought of which makes me want to die.

(For real.)

I head over to the cafeteria, where Cecily and Oliver are already eating at our table. I rush up next to them and plop down.

"What are you doing here?" Cecily squeals. "What about your test?"

"I have bad news," I reply. "My test has been postponed till tomorrow."

"Tomorrow *when*?" Oliver snipes, as if he already knows what's coming.

"Tomorrow . . . at ten-thirty A.M.?" I say, sheepishly. "I'm so, so, SO sorry! It's totally out of my control!"

"So you're just going to abandon us in our time of need?!" Oliver cries.

"I'm not abandoning you! But I have to take this exam, and it just happens to be during our performance. You two are going to have to hold down the fort without me."

"No!" Cecily and Oliver both scream in unison.

The whole lunch table turns to face us.

"Guys, it's going to be fine—I promise! You're both so good at this stuff, you have it all under control already. Really. You don't even need me."

"But you're the *president* of the club. You have to perform with us!" Oliver says.

"And you have no idea how much I wish I could," I say. And I mean it. "But I don't know what to do. I have to take this exam, and the examiners can't come till tomorrow."

The two of them just sit in silence with giant pouts on their faces.

"Look, you guys are going to do great without me!" I say, trying to sound chipper. "I completely trust you and I know you're going to make the Limbos proud. So, Ollie, as my VP, you are officially in charge of the Limbos' carnival event. I hand over my baton to you, okay?"

"Fine," he says, shifting from pouty to snooty.

My absolute favorite Oliver mood.

"You're going to do an amazing job!" I say once more, probably a little more for me than for them this time.

Just then, Kai joins us, having finally gotten herself some food. Oliver immediately breaks the bad news.

"This one is totally ditching us," he says after explaining the situation, pointing his finger at me in accusation. "Can you believe it?"

"That's a bummer," she says. "But I'm afraid I'm also the bearer of bad news. I'm definitely not doing my part, either. Guys, I totally suck at dancing as a ghost."

"OMG. Everything is completely falling apart!" Oliver cries out.

"No, everything's going to be okay," Cecily says calmly. "Allie can do your part easily, Kai. But you're still going to dance with us, right? We can definitely find a part for you—I promise."

"I'll dance if it makes sense and it doesn't mess anyone up," Kai says, "but I'm totally fine sitting this one out, too."

"Nonsense!" Oliver replies, slapping his hand on the table. "You're a Limbo now. And Limbos don't sit. They dance."

Watching them all come together to solve this puzzle and support one another gives me happy goose bumps up and down my arms. This? Is what friends do for one another. They support one another and go out of their way to make sure everyone feels included. That's the kind of friend I always want to be.

I think about how I treated Kai when she got here, and I immediately feel ashamed. Even though we're good now, I'm still sad about how things went down. I mean, think about it! She randomly wakes up dead one morning and arrives at this brand-new school. She doesn't know a soul. She can barely walk. And all she wants is for someone to be nice to her, to be her friend.

And then she meets me.

Welcome to Limbo!

I try to imagine what it would have been like for me if I hadn't had Cecily when I first crossed over, if I'd had to deal with this new place and being a ghost and Georgia, to boot, on top of it . . . *all by myself.*

Oh. My. Ghost.

I'm an awful person! No wonder the afterlife took the Limbos' performance away from me—I don't deserve it after the way I've acted. And the way I treated Lexi, like she was some leper—why? Just because I heard a rumor that she did something bad once. That's *not* the kind of person I want to be.

But wait. Slow your roll, Emotional Girl. Kai also forgave me! So there's hope for me yet.

(Right?)

Maybe, just maybe, when I apologize to Lexi, she'll forgive me too.

I need to dig down deep and figure out what it was that made me go all mean girl in the first place.

And then?

I need to clear out the blockage, like spring cleaning.

Or open-heart surgery.

Ghost Level Placement Examination

Name: Lucy Chadwick

Address: Limbo Central District, Jane Austen Cottage, Southampton Hall room 312

Counselor: Ms. Keaner, with assistance from Mr. Nasser

This examination will test your natural and supernatural abilities in the afterlife with written, oral, and performance portions to determine your natural aptitude for energy and matter manipulation. All answers, exhibitions, and results are final.

For examiners only:

Scores: Part 1 _____   Part 2 _____   Part 3 _____

Special Skills: _____
_____

Ghost Year Placement: _____

Chapter Nine
You May Begin

Okay, *now* the judgment day has come at last.

It's nine-thirty, which means I have just under an hour to find Lexi and Georgia to grovel for their forgiveness *and* stop by Stage A to make sure everything is in order for the Limbos' performance.

It's literally the least I can do.

I head over to Stage A first, and everything looks perfect. I stand in the middle of the stage, looking out at the would-be audience, thinking.

Last night we had a two-hour rehearsal to finalize the new parts. With me not being able to perform and Kai needing a new, less advanced role, we basically had to recast the whole last half of the piece on the last day.

It makes me think of all of those rehearsals I had back home before *The Nutcracker* performances and year-end recitals. Someone always got hurt at the last minute, or someone got the flu, and everything we'd spent months rehearsing for would completely unravel in a matter of seconds. One time, our Clara (basically the star of *The Nutcracker*'s first act) got snowed in on a flight back from visiting her grandparents in New York City!

Now, THAT was a nightmare.

Those nights always went down the same way. First there were tears. Lots and lots of tears. Then there was whispering about who was going to get the part that was suddenly now available. And finally, a decision was made, and everyone would stand up and get into position, ready to run through the piece as many times as it would take to make it perfect again.

Were those nights stressful? BEYOND.

But they were also magical.

It always amazed me to see everyone come together to make the impossible possible.

You know what they say—the show must go on, right?

Next, I head over to Stage B, where the cheer squad is

setting up, and spot Georgia and Lexi by the refreshment stand. I inch a bit closer to see what they're planning to sell and notice two giant plastic barrels, pump bottles filled with colored syrup, and boxes of straws. They're doing snow cones in little plastic football helmets!

Even *I* have to admit that's genius.

Lexi and Georgia are pretend fighting with a pair of plastic straws, *Star Wars*–style, when I get close enough for them to notice me.

"Hey," I say, but my voice cracks from nerves and it comes out all squeaky.

Perfect. That's *exactly* the tone I was going for: mouse.

"Seriously?" Georgia glares at me.

That must be her greeting of choice.

Lexi smirks at Georgia but doesn't say anything.

Tough crowd.

"Look," I continue, "I came because Kai told me the truth about why you guys were in the courtyard that night, and I wanted to say that I'm sorry I jumped to conclusions."

"I didn't quite hear you," Georgia replies, all snarky. "Could you repeat that for me?"

Deep breaths. In through the nose, out through the mouth. In through the nose, out through the—

"Give her a break, G," Lexi says. Then she turns to me. "Thanks for saying that."

"It's the least I could do," I reply. "I feel really bad that you were questioned all day yesterday because of me, and I'm sorry that I judged you just because of some dumb rumors I heard. I shouldn't have listened to them."

"Well, they weren't *all* rumors," Lexi says, bending her plastic straw in half. "I said you could believe *some* of them, remember? I *was* a part of that prank we pulled a couple years ago, but I didn't get expelled. I definitely got into trouble, but because it was only my first semester, my counselor thought it was mainly because I was hanging with the wrong kids. I was given the option to transfer to Limbo Central and start over again, and I took it."

"That's really cool of you," I say. "And thanks for telling me. You didn't have to. I mean, it's none of my business. But I'm glad I know now. I just wish I had listened to Miles earlier."

"Miles is a good guy," she says with a smile.

I try not to read too much into that. The memory of him

telling me that they used to date flies into my head, but I try to swat it away. I glance over to see what she has in her back pocket today, but she catches me in the act and gives me a weird look.

"It's just . . . you always carry a book," I explain. "I was just wondering what it was today."

She reaches around and pulls it from her jeans. "*Little Women*," she says with a smile.

"Are you finished?" Georgia barks, clearly irritated that Lexi and I have made amends. "We need to get to work."

"No, actually," I reply, "I'm not. I also owe *you* an apology."

I'm struggling to get the words out a little, but I remind myself it's all for a good cause!

I continue, "Kai's arrival made me realize how you must have felt when I showed up—"

"Oh, so it's *Kai's* fault, then?" Georgia cuts in.

"No, it's not Kai's fault," I reply, irritated. "I'm just saying . . . that I finally understand how jealousy and insecurity can make good people do pretty awful things. I've done a few of them myself this week. So, I just wanted to say that I get why you behaved the way you did toward me in the beginning, and I'm sorry about how it all went down."

Georgia looks at me like I've just jumped out of a fresh grave in the middle of the night.

Zombie-style.

"Uh-uh-okay," she stutters. "Fine. Thanks, I guess."

"You're welcome, I guess."

Well, THAT wasn't awkward or anything.

I smile at both of them. "By the way, this event idea is awesome," I say. "The football helmet snow cones are killer."

Before they can reply, I turn around and walk away.

I suddenly feel the awesome relief of all this weight lifted.

Well, some weight lifted.

There's still *something* there.

And it's dancing the jig on my chest.

The distance between Stage B and the administration office isn't that far, and since I still have some time before I have to report for my exam, I decide to take the long way around the other side of the school, where Miles and I took our walk that day during lunch. I think back to all the times we hung out this week—how comfortable it all felt.

Unlike all the times I've spent with Colin, which, well, let's put it this way: If the sound of nails on a chalkboard was a feeling, that's what LITERALLY every minute with Colin felt like this week.

EEK.

That thing still weighing on me? It has permanently moved into my brain and is currently spearing a "SOLD" sign on the front lawn of my amygdala.

It's something that Georgia said.

(Shocker, I know . . .)

When I mentioned Kai, she said, *"So it's Kai's fault, then?"* And that's got me thinking . . . why is it that when it comes to stuff like this, girls always blame one another? I mean, I didn't *think* I was blaming Kai, but I kind of was. Like, if she hadn't have come here, none of this would have happened. But . . . that's not entirely true, is it? I mean, the *reason* this whole situation turned into a replay of *Lucy and Georgia: The Early Years* isn't because Kai came to town, it's because of the way Colin *behaved* when Kai came to town.

Let's face it: If he hadn't started acting all shifty, if he had told me about Kai AND Kai about me, like a normal boyfriend, and hadn't stopped calling me at night or wanting to spend time together . . . if he hadn't brought her to our special place on the beach, or agreed to let her teach him how to surf, none of this would have happened! It's like I said earlier: He started doing all the things to me that he did to Georgia . . . and when you think about it, it's no wonder Georgia got all bent out of shape—and it's no wonder I did the same exact thing!

Boyfriends aren't supposed to make you feel all doubt-y and insecure, like they could just bolt the second something new and shiny comes along.

(At least, I *really* hope they aren't.)

(And Cecily says they aren't.)

(They aren't, right?)

I think back to my conversation with her a few days ago, and I realize the writing was on the wall the whole time.

Okay, it wasn't on *the* Wall.

But you know what I mean.

Sure, it's tough to find a groove in a new relationship, or whatever. But she told me that the moment Colin and I were alone together I would feel like myself again.

That all the doubt would fade away.

But the thing is? It hasn't.

And the reason it hasn't gone away has absolutely *nothing* to do with Kai or how beautiful and talented and totally cool she is, and absolutely EVERYTHING to do with the fact that Colin is a certified, giant, Class-A *dodo head*.

(To quote Cecily.)

My revelation is perfectly timed with my arrival at Ms. Keaner's office. She greets me at the door at ten-twenty and escorts me to Mr. Nasser's classroom, where the examiners are apparently already getting situated.

"How are you feeling this morning, Lucy?" she asks me as we walk through the hallway.

"Surprisingly confident," I say. And I mean it.

"Isn't that lovely to hear!" she sings. "Now, just do your best, dear, and don't worry about anything else."

We round the corner of Mr. Nasser's classroom, and I see three adults dressed in suits: two men, one woman. On the center desk sits one glowing Tabulator.

"Good morning," they say in unison, as we enter the room.

"Good morning," Ms. Keaner says. "This is Lucy Chadwick."

"Well, hello, Ms. Chadwick," the lady examiner says to me, holding out her hand for me to shake. "We've heard a lot about you."

"Thank you," I reply nervously.

"And I understand you have a carnival to get to," adds one of the men, "so perhaps we should get on with it?"

He motions for me to take a seat at the center desk with the Tabulator.

"Very well," Ms. Keaner says. "I'll be in my office, Lucy. Come find me when you're done."

"Thanks, Ms. Keaner," I reply, and head over to my seat.

"Now, Lucy," the man continues, "there are three parts to this examination: a written part, an oral part, and a performance part. The first part, as you can see, is the written portion. You have exactly forty-five minutes to complete this portion of the exam. Are you ready?"

"Yes," I reply.

"Very well, then. You may begin."

One hour and forty minutes later . . .

Ghost Level Placement Examination

Name: Lucy Chadwick

Address: Limbo Central District, Jane Austen Cottage, Southampton Hall room 312

Counselor: Ms. Keaner, with assistance from Mr. Nasser

This examination will test your natural and supernatural abilities in the afterlife with written, oral, and performance portions to determine your natural aptitude for energy and matter manipulation. All answers, exhibitions, and results are final.

For examiners only:

Scores: Part 1 ___94%___ Part 2 ___91%___ Part 3 ___99%___

Special Skills: *Ms. Chadwick is quite strong both emotionally and mentally, and can manipulate matter at a surprisingly evolved and advanced level for her crossover age. Her special skills consist of, but are not limited to: telepathy, advanced-level telekinesis, advanced light manipulation, and highly sophisticated matter manipulation.*

Ghost Year Placement:___Year 3___

"Year THREE!? This a joke, right? It's got to be a joke," I cry out in Ms. Keaner's office.

I'm staring at the Tabulator, where the examiners have written down their results, and even though it clearly states that ALL RESULTS ARE FINAL, I still can't believe what I'm seeing.

"Year Three, dear," she replies, smiling. "It's no joke. See, I knew you'd be great!"

"Okay, but Year Three? That means . . . I get to skip two full years of school?"

"Well, yes, in ghost levels. But your regular classes will remain the same."

"But what happens after . . . I mean, will I have to—"

"Lucy, dear, don't you worry about a thing," Ms. Keaner jumps in, trying to pull me back from my mental spiral downward. "School here is very different from what you're used to in the World of the Living. Everything is customized, not to mention that our standardized system goes all the way up to Year Six without any disruptions regarding location or districts. Everything is going to be just fine, I promise!"

A wave of relief rushes over me, and I finally start to get excited.

Ecstatic, actually.

But then I remember the Limbos' performance!

I glance at the clock, which reads 12:15 P.M.

"Is that really the time? I have to go!" I cry out, jumping out of my chair. "I have to try and catch the rest of the Limbos!"

"Of course, dear, you run off and have fun! And Lucy?"

"Yes?"

"Congratulations—we're so very proud of you!"

"Thanks, Ms. Keaner."

I sprint over to Stage A, hoping to catch at least the tail end of the performance, but when I get there it's completely empty! Is it over already? Did something happen?

OMG. What if no one showed up because everyone wanted to see the football players cheer instead?

Uh-oh. Cecily and Oliver will be crushed!

I sprint back over to Stage B to check out what's happening at cheer central.

"Oliver!" I call out, spotting him on the side down by the

front of the stage. "What's going on? How'd the performance go?"

"Lucy! You're here!" he cries out, and I see the rest of the Limbos turn around, including Cecily and Kai.

"I went over to Stage A first but it was empty. What happened?"

"First tell us how the exam went!" Cecily chimes in.

"It went really well," I say hesitantly.

"So?" Oliver prompts.

"Well, I got placed in Year Three."

"YEAR THREE!" they all cry in unison.

"Shhhh," I say, laughing. "Yes. *Now* tell me what you guys are all doing here?"

"We simply couldn't perform without our prez," Oliver tells me, putting his arms around me. "Principal Tilly helped us move some things around so we could have the stage at 2:30. And since we're not performing, we came over here to support the cheer squad."

"You moved the performance for me?" I say, shocked. "I can't believe you would do that!"

This? Is the second unbelievable thing I've heard in the last twenty minutes.

It's been a pretty good twenty minutes, all in all.

"I, for one, can't think of a better reason to move it," Oliver replies.

"Me neither!" Cecily seconds.

"Me three!" Kai adds.

Just then, Colin appears by my side.

"Hey," he says. "Can we talk for a sec?"

"Sure."

We move away from the crowd over to the side of the stage.

"I just wanted to say again that I'm really sorry for the way I've been acting," Colin says, sincerely. "I never should have taken Kai to the beach, and I should have told her about you—all the things you said I shouldn't have done, well, you were right. I just . . . I really like you, Lucy, and I want things to go back to normal. Can we just forget all about this week and move on?"

I take a deep breath. This? Is going to be hard.

"Thanks for saying all that," I begin. "You're right—you were a total dodo head."

"Dodo head?" he repeats.

"Yes! *Dodo head.*"

We both have to laugh at that.

"And I do accept your apology. *Apologies*, actually. But . . . " I continue, "I think we both just jumped into this whole thing a little too quickly. You went from Georgia to me, and I really liked you, so I said yes, but I don't think I really knew what this whole dating thing meant. I don't know if I'm ready for it all. And I'm not sure you are, either."

"Is it because you're still thinking about Miles?"

"What? I'm not . . . It's not—"

"Lucy, I don't have to be telepathic to know that he's on your mind."

"You're right. I'm sorry," I say, finally.

Because he *is* right. Miles is on my mind, and he has been this whole time. And that? Is on me.

"I think the fact that your behavior around Kai makes me feel bad about myself, and my connection with Miles makes you feel bad about yourself means that this thing isn't right."

"Maybe," he says.

"Anyway, I have a lot to focus on now, with school and my new ghost level, and I think it would be best if . . . if we went back to being just friends. No hard feelings."

"Right," he replies. But I can tell he's disappointed.

We stand there in silence for a few seconds, and even though breakups are totally THE WORST, I have to admit this is the first time all week that I've actually felt like me.

Welcome home, Lucy.

Don't forget to return your seat and tray table into their upright and locked positions.

"So," he continues, breaking through the quiet. "What level did you place into?"

"Year Three."

"Whoa! Year Three? That's amazing! Not that I'm surprised."

"Thanks."

"I guess you and Miles are going to be spending a lot more time together now, huh?"

"We're just friends," I reply, and hope that he believes me.

"I know. Just like us."

I suddenly remember the necklace he gave me last week before the play, and I reach around my neck to unhook it.

"Here," I say, trying to work out the clasp, "you should have this back. It's really beautiful, but I don't think I should keep it."

"It's a good luck charm," he says, holding his hand up to stop me. "I gave it to you for good luck, and now that you're skipping two ghost years, you're really going to need it!"

"Ha-ha, very funny."

"Players, it's that time!" we hear Georgia yell into the crowd. "Take your places, NOW!"

"Well, I better go," Colin says. "Before Georgia has my head."

"So *that's* what the helmets are for!" I joke as he runs off.

And THAT, my friends, is how to lose your first boyfriend in less than eight short days.

This kind of magic? Takes skill, people. I believe it's referred to as "highly sophisticated matter manipulation."

At least that's what the experts are calling it.

At 2:20 P.M., we all head over to Stage A for the Limbos' performance.

Take two.

The cheer event was awesome, and they had a great turn-out. And you know what? It was actually really fun watching Colin and the rest of the football team cheer. They were hilarious, and everyone had a blast. In fact, I think it's been one of the most popular events so far.

Which means the Limbos really have to BRING IT.

"Okay, Limbos!" I say as we huddle up right before we take our places. "The most important thing is to have fun out there! I know you're all going to do great. Just smile and have a blast."

"And stay in your formations and pay attention to the people around you!" Oliver barks.

"Dude, take it down a notch," I say, laughing. "But yes, definitely make eye contact and connect with your fellow Limbo members on stage. After all, this isn't a solo piece—we've all got to work together. Ready? Let's get out there and show them what the Limbos are made of!"

Just as we're getting into position, I spot Miles in the audience.

Our eyes lock.

Again.

You were right, I think at him. *I should have trusted you.*

*Well, you never fail to point out how
much older and wiser I am.*

Not for long. Guess who just got placed in Year Three?

Miles's eyes open so big it looks like they might pop out of their sockets. Then a wide grin spreads across his face.

*Hmmm . . . I guess I was right after all.
There's really not much of an age difference
between us anymore.*

So it would seem.

Just then, the music starts.

Break a leg.

I suddenly feel butterflies inside my stomach—the kind I always used to get back home right before a performance.

There's just something about the feel of the crowd when you're on stage, and the energy that runs through your veins when you're out there flying free. It's like . . . I don't know, like Emotional Girl finally gets to come out of her shell.

Without the whole uncontrolled violence factor.

There are a few fumbles here and there from all the part-switching we did, but overall the performance is a total smash!

Afterward, I see Mia standing next to Stacy Francis by the refreshments, and walk over to her.

"Hi," I say, quietly. "Thanks for coming."

"Of course I came—I wouldn't miss it."

"I just . . . I want to make sure we're okay," I say.

"We're more than okay, Lucy," she says. "You didn't do anything wrong. You told me what you saw, and the fact is you were right. What I did, pushing that article through without making absolutely sure it was *all* true—that's my bad."

"Still, if there's anything I can do to help make things better, you know, with *her*," I say, motioning toward Stacy, "just say the word."

"I will," she says. "You know, I heard the carnival committee talking after the performance, and I think you've got a really good chance of winning."

"You think?"

"Yup. They totally DIED over your rendition of the school song!"

"Ha-ha," I say.

"I'm serious though. They dug it."

"Well, I owe all of my *school spirit* to Kai."

I guess that's the thing about friends. No matter what happens in life—or afterlife—good or bad, they're always there to raise your spirits.

Let's just say, for the sake of argument, that you do something dumb and get into serious trouble at school . . . you falsely accuse a student of theft in the school newspaper *by accident*, or you're overwhelmed about an important test you have to take . . . maybe you even, oh, I don't know . . . break up with your boyfriend?

Friends—good friends—will *always* be there.

With spirit bells on.

BREAKING NEWS FROM THE LIMBOLATER...

SCHOOL SPIRIT TIES RUN DEEP

By Mia Bennett*

It's a tie! That's right, folks. And after two long years of holding a Spirit grudge against North Limbo, *The Limbolater* is overjoyed to announce that both winners of the Limbo Spirit Cup proudly preside squarely in the Limbo Central School District.

At just after 5:30 P.M. the Saturday of this year's carnival, the carnival committee convened to determine the winner, and emerged from their chambers only ten minutes after entering it.

The verdict? The winners of the Cup are none other than Limbo Central's cheerleading squad leader, Georgia Sinclaire, AND Limbo Central's newest club president of the Limbos dance troupe, Lucy Chadwick!

"It was by far the most original use of the school song we've ever witnessed," said a member of the committee, referring to the Limbos' use of the Limbo Central school song, "Upon Yonder Hills."

---

* Disclaimer: This article was written by Mia Bennett at the behest of the Limbo Spirit Carnival winners. Editor in chief Stacy Francis IS NOT affiliated with this article in any way, nor does she approve of its inclusion in said issue of The Limbolater.

"And the cooperation of the cheer squad and the football team was the very definition of school spirit in my book!" said another committee member, of the innovative and entertaining decision to have the Limbo Central football players perform a well-known cheer routine for the masses.

"This exhibition of camaraderie, inclusiveness, and spirit is exactly what we encourage here at Limbo Central," Principal Tilly told us later on that day, "and I, for one, am extremely proud of each and every one of my students."

As you may recall, the winners of the Cup are offered a certain percentage of the funds earned at the carnival to designate toward their chosen club or cause of choice.

When asked what they each plan to do with the earnings, the Cup winners had this to say:

"Obviously, the money will go toward the cheer squad," Ms. Sinclaire replied, matter-of-factly. "We *really* need new uniforms."

Ms. Chadwick seemed just as convinced that her choice was the *only* choice: "The Limbos are a brand-new club, unlike some of the other clubs—the cheer squad, for example—that have been around for *ages*. So the earnings would be best spent going toward props and costumes for our next performance!"

Perhaps these two ladies will have an easier time agreeing on where to display the Spirit Cup?

Whether Limbo Central gets new

cheerleader uniforms or new Limbos costumes remains to be seen, but one thing we can be certain of is this: The school spirit ties to Limbo Central Middle School run deep—among students, among faculty members, and of course, among friends.

Don't miss a minute in Limbo!

Happily Ever Afterlife #1:
Ghostcoming!

Happily Ever Afterlife #2:
Crushed

Happily Ever Afterlife #3:
Drama

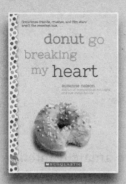

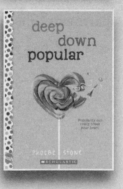

Orli Zuravicky is a writer, an editor, and an amateur interior designer, which basically means she likes to paint stuff in her apartment. She has been in children's publishing for fifteen years and has written over sixty-five books for children. She hopes to write sixty-five more. She lives her happily ever after (life) in Brooklyn, New York.